Literature of Mystery and Detection

THE
NOTTING HILL MYSTERY

[Charles Felix]

ARNO PRESS
A New York Times Company
1976

Editorial Supervision: EVE NELSON

Reprint Edition 1976 by Arno Press Inc.

LITERATURE OF MYSTERY AND DETECTION
ISBN for complete set: 0-405-07860-9
See last pages of this volume for titles.

Manufactured in the United States of America

Library of Congress Cataloging in Publication Data

Felix, Charles.
    The Notting Hill mystery.

    (Literature of mystery and detection)
    Reprinted from the 1945 ed. of M. L. Richardson's
Novels of mystery from the Victorian age, published
by Pilot Press, London.
    I. Title. II. Series.
PZ3.F334No5   [PR4699.F183]   823'.8   75-32744
ISBN 0-405-07870-6

THE
NOTTING HILL MYSTERY

THE NOTTING HILL MYSTERY

Mr. R. Henderson to the Secretary of the . . . Life Assurance Association.

Private Enquiry Office,
Clement's Inn.
17th Jan., 1858.

" Gentlemen,

In laying before you the extraordinary revelations arising from my examination into the case of the late Madame . . ., I have to apologise for the delay in carrying out your instructions of November last. It has been occasioned, not by any neglect on my part, but by the unexpected extent and intricacy of the enquiry into which I have been led. I confess that after this minute and laborious investigation I could still have wished a more satisfactory result, but a perusal of the accompanying documents, on the accuracy and completeness of which you may fully rely, will I doubt not fully satisfy you of the unusual difficulty of the case.

My enquiries have had reference to a policy of assurance for £5,000, the maximum amount permitted by your rules, on the life of the late Madame **, effected in your office by her husband, the Baron R**, and bearing date 1st November, 1855. Similar policies were held in the . . . of Manchester, the . . . of Liverpool, the . . . of Edinburgh, and the . . . of Dublin, the whole amounting to £25,000 ; the dates, 23rd December, 1855, 10th January, 25th January, and 15th February, 1856, respectively, being in effect almost identical. These companies joined in the instructions under which I have been acting ; and from the voluminous nature of this letter and its enclosures, I shall be obliged by your considering my present reply as addressed to them conjointly with yourselves.

Before entering upon the subject of my investigations, it may be as well to recapitulate the circumstances under which they were originated. Of these the first was the coincidence of dates, above noticed ; and an apparent desire on the part of the assurer to conceal from each of the various offices the fact of similar policies having been elsewhere simultaneously effected. On examining further into the matter your Board was also struck with the peculiar conditions under which the marriage appeared to have taken place, and the relation in which Madame R** had formerly stood to the Baron. To these points, therefore, my attention was specially directed, and the facts thus elicited form a very important link in the singular chain of evidence I have been enabled to put together.

The chief element of suspicion, however, was to be found in the very unusual circumstances attendant on the death of Madame R**, especially following so speedily as it did on the assurance for so large an aggregate amount. This lady died suddenly on the 15th March,

475

1857, from the effects of a powerful acid taken, it is supposed, in her sleep, from her husband's laboratory. In the Baron's answers to the usual preliminary enquiries, forwarded for my assistance, and herewity returned, there is no admission of any propensity to somnambulism· Shortly, however, after the occurrence had been noticed in the public prints, a letter to the Secretary of the Association from a gentleman recently lodging in the same house with Baron R**, gave reason to suspect that, in this respect, at least, some concealment had been practised, and the matter was then placed in my hands.

On receipt of your instructions, I at once put myself in communication with Mr. Aldridge, the writer of the letter in question. That gentleman's evidence certainly goes to show that, within at least a very few months after the date of the latest policy, Baron R** was not only himself aware of such a propensity in his wife, but desirous of concealing it from others. Mr. Aldridge's statements are also to a certain extent supported by those of two other witnesses ; but, unfortunately, there are, as will be seen, circumstances calculated to throw considerable doubt upon the whole of this evidence, and especially on that of Mr. Aldridge, from which alone the more important part of the inference is drawn. The same must, unfortunately, be said with regard to some other parts of the evidence, as will be more clearly seen when the case itself is before you.

From his statement, however, in conjunction with other circumstances, I learned enough to induce me to extend my researches to another very singular case, which not long since had given rise to considerable comment.

You will, no doubt, remember that in the autumn of 1856 a gentleman of the name of Anderton was arrested on suspicion of having poisoned his wife, and that he committed suicide whilst awaiting the issue of a chemical enquiry into the cause of her death. This enquiry resulted in an acquittal, no traces of the suspected poison being found ; and the affair was hushed up as speedily as possible, many of Mr. Anderton's connections being of high standing in society, and naturally anxious for the honour of the family. I must, however, acknowledge the readiness with which, in the interest of justice, I have been furnished by them with every facility for pushing my enquiries, the results of which are now before you.

In reviewing the whole facts, and more especially the series of remarkable coincidences of dates, etc., to which I beg to direct your most particular attention, two alternatives present themselves. In the first we must altogether ignore a chain of circumstantial evidence so complete and close-fitting in every respect, as it seems almost impossible to disregard ; in the second we are inevitably led to a conclusion so at variance with all the most firmly established laws of nature, as it seems almost equally impossible to accept. The one leaves us precisely at the point from which we started ; the other involves the imputation of a series of most horrible and complicated crimes.

Between these alternatives I am constrained to confess my own inability, after long and careful study, to decide. I have determined, therefore, simply to submit for your consideration the facts of the case as they appear in the depositions of the several parties from whom my information has been obtained. These I have arranged, as far as possible, in the form in which they would be laid before counsel, should it ultimately be deemed advisable to bring the affair into Court. In view, however, of the extreme length of the case, I have given, in a condensed form, the substance of such of the depositions as did not seem likely to suffer from such treatment. The more important I have left to tell their own tale, and, in any case, my abstract may be at once checked by the originals, all of which are enclosed.

Should your conclusions be such as have been forced upon myself, further deliberation will yet be required with reference to the course to be pursued ; a point on which, in such case, I confess myself almost equally unable to advise. Whether, in a matter so surrounded with suspicion, it might not be well, in any event, to resist the claim, is certainly a question to be considered. On the other hand, even assuming the fullest proof of the terrible crimes involved, it is a matter calling for no less careful consideration, whether they would be found of a nature to bring the criminal within reach of the law. For the present, however, our concern is with the facts of the case, and ulterior questions had better be left on one side till that issue is decided, when, I conclude, I shall hear further from you on the subject.

In conclusion, I must trouble you with a few words on a point which seems to require explanation. I allude to the apparent prominence I have been compelled to afford to the workings of what is called ' Mesmeric Agency.' Those, indeed, who are so unfortunate as to be the victims of this delusion, would doubtless find in it a simple, though terrible, solution of the mystery we are endeavouring to solve. But while frankly admitting that it was the passage from the ' Zoist Magazine,' quoted in the course of the evidence, which first suggested to my mind the only conclusion I have as yet been able to imagine, I beg at the outset most distinctly to state, that I would rather admit my own researches to have been baffled by an illusory coincidence, than lay myself open to giving the slightest credit to that impudent imposture. We must not, however, forget that those whose lives have been passed in the deception of others, not unfrequently end by deceiving themselves. There is, therefore, nothing incredible in the idea that the Baron R** may have given sufficient credence to the statement of the 'Zoist,' abovementioned, for the suggestion to his own mind of a design, which by the working of a true, though most mysterious law of Nature, may really have been carried out. Such, at least, is the only theory by which I can attempt, in any way, to elucidate this otherwise unfathomable mystery.

Awaiting the honour of your further commands,

I am, Gentlemen, very faithfully yours,

RALPH HENDERSON."

SECTION I. THE CASE

Extracts from the Correspondence of the Hon. Catherine B**.

1—*From Lady Bolton to the Hon. C. B** (undated), about October or November of 1832.**

" Oh, auntie, auntie, what shall I do ? For three nights I have not closed my eyes, and I would not write even to you, auntie dear, because I kept hoping that, after all, things might come right, and he would come back again. Oh, how I have listened to every sound, and watched the road till my poor eyes ache ! And now this is the fourth day since he went away, and oh, auntie, I am so frightened, for I am sure he is gone after that dreadful man, and oh, if he should meet him, I know something terrible will happen, for you can't tell how he looked, poor Edward, I mean, when he went away. But, indeed, auntie, you must not be angry with him, for I know it was all my own fault, for I ought to have told him everything long ago, though indeed, indeed, I never cared for him, and I do love dear Edward so dearly. I was afraid. . . .

(Here the MS. becomes in places very blotted and illegible).

and I thought it was all at an end, and then . . . and only a fortnight ago we were so happy . . . married hardly seven months and . . . but you must not think I am complaining of him, dear Auntie, for you don't know how. . . . Only, if you can, come to me, for I feel getting so ill, and you know it is only. . . . God bless you, auntie ; oh, do come to me if you can.

GERTRUDE BOLTON."

2—*Extract of letter from the Same to the Same, written about four days later.*

" I am so sorry to hear you are so ill ; don't try to come, darling auntie ; I shall do somehow, and if not, anything is better than this horrible suspense. . . . No tidings, yet but I cannot write more, for I can hardly see to guide the pen, and my poor head seems to open and shut. God bless you, auntie.

G."

" I open my letter to thank you so much for sending dear kind Mrs. Ward ; she came in so unexpectedly (in a blue)† just as if she had come from heaven. I wonder if she has seen Ed. . . ."

(Here the MS. ends suddenly).

---

* Great-aunt of the late Mrs. Anderton. The object of going so far back will presently appear.

† Scratched out.

3—*From Mrs. Ward to Hon. C. B**, enclosing the above.*

Beechwood,* Tuesday Night.

" My dear Catherine,

I fear I have but a poor account to give you of our dear Gertrude. Poor child, when I came into the room, and saw her looking so pale and wan, and with great black circles round her eyes, I could scarcely keep in my own tears. She gave a little cry of joy when she saw me, and threw herself upon my neck ; but a moment after, turned to the writing table and tore open the letter I send you with this, and which was lying ready for the post. The long-continued strain seems to have been too much for her, and she had hardly written a line when her head began to wander, as you will see from the conclusion of her postscript, and in trying to write her husband's name she broke down altogether, and went off into a fit of hysterics which lasted for several hours. She is now, I am thankful to say, comparatively calm again, though at time her head still wanders, and she seems quite unable to close her eyes, but lies in her bed looking straight before her, and occasionally talking to herself in a low voice, but without seeming to notice anything. I have endeavoured, as far as I dared, to draw from her the history of this sad affair, but can get nothing, poor child, but eager assurances that it was ' all her fault,' and that ' indeed, indeed, *he* was not to blame.' It seems as though my coming—though certainly a great relief to her—had had the effect of putting her on her guard lest anything should escape her unfavourable to her husband, and her whole faculties seem to be concentrated in the endeavour to shield him from reproach. I fear, however, there can be no doubt that he has been very seriously to blame ; indeed, from all I can gather, the fault seems to have been entirely on his side. What is the precise history of this unhappy business I have not been able to learn ; but it seems that Sir Edward, who is certainly a most violent young man, and I fear also of a most jealous temperament, contracted some suspicion with regard to that Mr. Hawker who so perseveringly persecuted poor Gertrude the winter before last, and to have left Beechwood, after a very distressing scene, in pursuit of him. Mr. Hawker is supposed to be on the Continent, and it is known that Sir Edward took the Dover Road, which, as you know, passes close by this place. This is all I can at present learn with any certainty, though I hear but too much from the servants, who are all in such a state of indignation at Sir Edward's treatment of their mistress, that I have the utmost difficulty in re-straining it from finding some open vent. Should I hear more, I will of course let you know at once ; but meanwhile I cannot conceal from you my deep anxiety for our dear Gertrude, whose poor little heart seems quite broken, and for whom I am in hourly dread of the effect but too likely to be produced, in her present delicate state, by the anxiety and terror from which she is suffering. . . . You know how much I always disliked the match, and I feel more than ever the

* The residence of Sir Edward Bolton.

impropriety of consigning so young and sensitive a girl to the care of a man of such notoriously uncontrollable temper. Poor thing! This is evidently not the first time she has suffered from it, and, even should she herself escape without permanent injury to her constitution, I dread the effect upon the child. . . . And now I must close this long and sad letter, but will write again should anything fresh occur; meantime, I cannot be longer away from Gertrude's side. I hope your own health is improving. My love to little Henry, and tell him to be very good while I am away.

Your affectionate,

HELEN WARD."

4—*The Same to the Same.*

Beechwood, Monday morning.

" My dear Catherine,

I am sorry to say I can still send you no better account of poor Gertrude. Since I last wrote, by Saturday evening's post* very little change has taken place, though she is certainly more restless, poor child, and I fear also, if anything, weaker. She now constantly asks for letters, and seems impressed with the idea that we are keeping them from her, as indeed, in her present state, I should, I think, take the responsibility of doing, if any arrived. The newspaper I have always kept from her until it has first been carefully examined. I am dreading fever, though by the doctor's advice I have not attempted to dissuade her from getting up. The exertion, however, is almost more than she can bear, and I am looking anxiously for his next visit. She lies all day on the sofa, looking out of the window, which commands a view of the Dover Road. This morning she seems growing more and more restless, and I am waiting with inexpressible anxiety for Dr. Travers.

Eleven o'clock.

The doctor has been, and confirms my fear of approaching fever, which, however, he says may possibly pass off. He has ordered me to lie down at once for some hours, as I have hardly been in bed since I arrived, and he says if fever should come on I shall want all the strength I can get. I shall keep this letter open, to send you by the evening's post the latest account.

Wednesday.

All is over. I can hardly command myself sufficiently to write, and yet I must tell you what has happened. Oh, my dear Catherine, how shall I ever forgive myself for leaving poor dear Gertrude; and yet I know that this is foolish, for I was ordered to do so for her sake. But I must come at once to the sad news I have to tell. I left poor Gertrude in the charge of her maid, with strict injunctions to call me if there should be any change; but the poor child seems to have grown quieter, and at length to have fallen asleep. The maid watched her until just four o'clock, when, overcome with weariness, she herself

This letter is omitted as containing nothing of any importance.

dropped off into a doze, and on waking at a little before five, was horrified to find herself alone. She flew at once to me, but I had hardly got to the top of the stairs when some one came running up to say that the postman was below, and had just met with poor Gertrude, who had been watching for him at the gate. She enquired eagerly after letters, and on being told there were none, asked for the newspaper, which she at once hurried away with into a part of the grounds called the Wilderness, while the postman, fearing from her manner that there was something amiss, came on to the house to tell what had occurred. I need not tell you with what anxiety I hastened to the Wilderness, and there, poor girl, we found her, stretched upon the turf close by the edge of the lake, with the fatal newspaper in her hand. I had her taken carefully to the house, and a man despatched on horseback for the doctor ; but before he arrived she had recovered consciousness, only, poor child, to be seized at once with the signs of her approaching trouble. From that moment until she breathed her last—an hour ago —I have never left her side. After nearly thirty hours of the most terrible suffering I have ever witnessed, she at length gave birth to two poor little girls, both so small and weak-looking that it was quite piteous to see them. The elder in especial, which was born about an hour before the second, is so weak and sickly, that the doctor says it is scarcely possible it can live, and, indeed, one can hardly hope that it may. The second seems stronger, but both are very small and weakly even considering their premature birth.

Poor Gertrude now sank rapidly, and though every means was tried, and she still lingered on for three or four hours, she at last sank altogether, passing away at the last so quietly that we hardly knew she was gone. Poor darling, I always loved her as being such a favourite with you all. . . . One word before I close as to the paper which was the unhappy cause of this terrible blow. It contained, as I had feared, the long-dreaded intelligence of Sir Edward's fatal quarrel with Mr. H. ; and I send it off by the same post, as you will wish to know the sad particulars. I cannot write more now, for I am fairly worn out, and must take some rest. You know how deeply I sympathise with you. . . .

Most affectionately yours,

HELEN WARD."

5—*Extract from " The Morning Herald," of the 12th of November,* 1832.

Fatal Duel at Dieppe.—We learn from the Paris papers, that an extraordinary and fatal duel took place some days since in the neighbourhood of Dieppe, between two Englishmen, neither of whom has as yet been identified. It appears that the parties encountered each other in the court-yard of the Hotel de l'Europe, where one of them, whose linen bears the mark of C.G.H., had been staying for some days. The new-comer at once assailed the other evidently with the most opprobrious language, to which Mr. H. replied with equal warmth, but the conversation being carried on in English, was unfortunately not understood by any one present. The altercation at length grew so warm that the landlord was compelled to interfere, and the parties then left the hotel together. A few hours afterwards, Mr. H. returned, and calling for his bill, hastily packed his portmanteau and departed. He has since been traced to Paris, where he was lost sight of altogether. Early the next morning a rumour spread that the body of an Englishman had been found in a vineyard, about a mile distant from the town, and on enquiry it proved that the victim was no other than the gentleman with whom the dispute had occurred on the previous night. It was evident on examination that the unfortunate man must have fallen in fair fight, though no seconds appear to have been present during the encounter. A pistol, recently discharged, was firmly grasped in the hand of the dead man ; and at a dozen paces lay its fellow, evidently the weapon with which he had been killed. The fatal wound, too, was exactly in that portion of the chest which would be exposed to an adversary's fire, and had evidently pierced the heart, so that death must have been instantaneous. The weapons, too, with which the fatal duel was fought appear to have been the property of the deceased. They were a very handsome pair of duelling pistols, hair triggers, evidently of English make. On the butt of each was a small silver shield, bearing the initials " E.B." and an armed hand grasping a crossbow. The initials of the unfortunate gentleman's opponent were, as we have said, C.G.H. ; and we have reason to fear that the victim was a young baronet, of considerable landed property, with whose sudden departure for the Continent rumour has for some time been busy.

Since our first edition went to press, we have received further particulars, which leave no room to doubt that the victim of the above fatal occurrence was, as we feared, Sir Edward Bolton, Bart., of Beechwood, Kent ; but the cause of the duel, and the name of his opponent, still remain a mystery. The unfortunate gentleman leaves behind him a young wife, to whom he was united but a few months since. Failing a male heir, the baronetcy will now, we understand, become extinct, while the bulk of the estates will pass to a distant connection. The widow, however, is, we believe, in possession of a considerable independent property.

6—*Mrs. Ward to Hon. C.B**.*

July, 1836.

" My dear Catherine,

You ask me whether I am satisfied with what I saw the other day of poor Gertrude Bolton's little ones. To say that I am satisfied with their appearance would, poor little things, be hardly true, for they are still anything but healthy—poor Gertie especially looking like a faded lily. The younger, however, is certainly improved, and will, I hope, do well, and I quite think that they both are better where they are than they could possibly be elsewhere. It is indeed sad, poor things, that they should have no near relation with whom they could live, but I quite agree with you, that in your state of health, it would not only be too great an undertaking for yourself, but would be by no means beneficial to them. Indeed I am convinced that on every account they are best where they are. The air of Hastings seems to suit them, and in the higher part of the town where Mrs. Taylor lives is bracing without being too cold. Mrs. Taylor herself is a most excellent person, and extremely fond of them. She seems especially interested in poor Gertie, and never wearies of relating instances of the wonderful sympathy between the twins. This sympathy seems even more physical than mental. According to Mrs. Taylor, every little ailment that affects the one is immediately felt by the other also, though with this difference, that your namesake, Katie, is but very slightly affected by Gertie's troubles, while she, poor child, I suppose from the greater delicacy of her constitution, is rendered seriously ill by every little indisposition of her sister. I have often heard of the strong physical sympathies between twins, but never met myself with so marked an instance. Both unfortunately are sadly nervous, though here, too, the elder is the greatest sufferer, while in the younger, it seems to take the form of extreme quickness of perception. . . . Of course, as they grow up, they should be placed with someone in their own rank of life, but for the present I think poor Mrs. Taylor will do very well. . . . I shall be at Hastings again next month, and will write when I have seen them.

Affectionately yours,

HELEN WARD."

7—*From Mrs. Taylor to Hon. C. B***.

About January, 1837.

" Honnered Miss,

With My Humbel duty to Your ladyshipp and i am trewly sory to sai as mis Gerterud hav took a terrabel bad cold wich i was afeard on as she wud do has Miss Kattarren av Likeways Had wun for 2 dais past wich i Am sory to sai as mis gerterud is wuss than mis Kattaren but Hoping she wil be Well agan Sone wich has I hev told your Honnered Ladyship they as allers the same trubbels ony pore mis gerterud allers hav them Wust. Honnered Miss the docto have ben her wich he sais his mis Katteren his quite wel agen he said Honnered mis he hops mis gerterud will sone be wel 2. honnered Mis yore Humbel servt. to command

SARAH TAYLER."

8—From the Same to the Same.

about June, 1837.

" Honnered Mis

with My humbel Duty to Yore ladyshipp hand i am trewly thenkfull
to sai the dere childern are both quit wel wich miss Kattaren made
erself Hill on teusday and pore miss gerterud were verry bade in
consekens for 3 dais but his now quit wel agen. Honnored mis yore
Ladyshipps humbel servt. to command

SARAH TAYLER."

9—From Same to Same.

July, 1837.

" Honnered Mis

with my humbel duty to Yore ladyshipp hand wud you please Cum
Direcly wich sumthink Dredfull hav apenned to pore mis Kattaren
honnered mis Yor Ladyshipps humbel servt. to comand

SARAH TAYLER."

10—Mr. Ward to Hon. C. B**.

Marine Hotel, Hastings.

12th July, 1837.

Dear Miss B**,

Helen was unfortunately prevented from leaving home at the time
your letter arrived, so, as the matter seemed urgent, I thought it best
to come myself. I am sorry to have to send you such very unsatisfactory intelligence. Poor little Catherine has been lost—stolen, I am
afraid, by gipsies—and I have hitherto been quite unable to find any
clue to their whereabouts. It appears that Mrs. Taylor took them
with some friends of hers for a trip to Fairlie Down, where they fell
in with a gang of gipsies, of whom, however, they did not take any
particular notice. They had taken their dinner with them, and after
finishing it sat talking for some time, when suddenly the child was
missed ; and, though they hunted in every direction for several hours,
no trace of her could be found. On returning to the place where the
gipsies had been seen, the camp was found broken up, and the track,
after passing near where they had been sitting, was lost on the hard
road. Unfortunately, poor Mrs. Taylor—who seems quite distracted
by what has happened—could think of nothing at first but writing to
you, and it was only by the gossip of her friends, who live at some
distance from the town, that the intelligence at length reached the
police. Enquiries were being set on foot when I arrived last night,
but I fear that, from the time that has been lost, there is now but little
chance of recovering the poor child. I have advertised in all directions,
and offered a large reward, but I have little hope of the result, nor are
the police more sanguine tham myself. Unfortunately poor Catherine's
dark, gipsy-like complexion, and black eyes and hair, will render it easy
to disguise her features, while her quick intelligence, and lithe, active

figure, will make her only too valuable an acquisition to the band. I
need not tell you how grieved I am at this fresh trouble to these poor
children, and I fear Gertrude will suffer severely from the loss of her
sister, with whom she has, as you know, so extraordinary a bond
of sympathy. I am going now to the police station, to consult on
further measures, and will write to you again by to-morrow morning's
post.

Ever, dear Miss B**,
Very truly yours,
HENRY WARD."

11—*Mrs. Vansittart to the Hon. C. B**.*

Grove Hill House Academy,
Hampstead Heath,
Wednesday, May 1st, 1842.

" Madam,
I have much pleasure in complying with your request for a monthly
report of the health and progress of my very interesting young friend
and pupil, Miss Bolton. In a moral and educational point of view
nothing could possibly be more satisfactory. . .   Of my dear you ng
friend's health I am compelled, however, to lament my inability to
address you in the same congratulatory terms which in all other matters
I am happily so well authorised to employ. Notwithstanding the
extreme salubrity of the atmosphere by which in this justly celebrated
locality she is surrounded, and I trust I may venture to add the un-
remitting attention she has experienced both at my own hands and
those of my medical and educational assistants, her general health is
still, I regret to say, very far from having attained to that condition of
entire convalescence at which I trust she may yet, with the advantage
of a prolonged residence upon the Heath, before very long arrive.
My medical adviser, Dr. Winstanley—a physician of European reputation, and one in whom I can repose the most entire confidence—in-
forms me that Miss Bolton is suffering from no especial ailment,
though subject from time to time to fits of illness to which it is often
difficult to assign any sufficient cause, and which after a while disappear
as strangely as they arose. He trusts with me that the pure air of the
Heath, which so far as we can venture to believe has already been
beneficial to his interesting patient, will in course of time effect a
radical cure. The loss of her young sister of which you informed me
on her first joining our little society, inflicted, beyond doubt, a very
serious blow upon her naturally feeble constitution; but I trust that
its effects are already passing away. I shall, of course, adhere strictly
to your instructions never in any way to allude to the sad occurrence
in conversation with Miss Bolton, and have thought it advisable not
to acquaint her companions with the fact. On the 1st of next month
I shall again do myself the honour of acquainting you with the progress
made by my interesting young friend, and have little doubt of being

able at that time to furnish you with a satisfactory account of her physical no less than of her moral and intellectual advancement. For the present, dear Madam, permit me to subscribe myself,

Yours very faithful,
And obliged servant,
Amelia Dorothea Vansittart.

" To the Hon. Catherine B★★."

12—*Mrs. Ward to the Hon. C. B★★.*

14th June, 1851.

" My dear Catherine,

Very many thanks for your early intelligence of dear Gertrude's engagement. I congratulate you most heartily, though as you have yourself alluded to it, I cannot deny that I should have been better pleased had Mr. Anderton, in addition to all his other good qualities, possessed that of a somewhat less nervous and excitable temperament. I have always liked him much ; but with poor Gertrude's own delicate constitution I cannot but fear the results of such an union upon both. However, it is impossible to have everything, and in all other respects he seems more than unexceptionable, so once more I congratulate you heartily. Are you really thinking of coming up to the Exhibition? . . . Give my best love to dear Gertrude, and say all that is kind and proper for us to her *fiancé*. Ever, dear Catherine,

Affectionately yours,
HELEN WARD."

SECTION II

1—*Memorandum by Mr. Henderson.*

We now come to that portion of Mrs. Anderton's* history which embraces the period between her marriage and the commencement of her last illness. For this I have been compelled to have recourse to various quarters. The information thus afforded is very complete, and taken in conjunction with what we have already seen in Miss B——'s correspondence of the previous life of this unfortunate lady, throws considerable light upon two important points to be hereafter noticed. The depositions, however, unavoidably run to a greater length than at this stage of the proceedings, their bearing on the main points of the case would render necessary, and I have therefore condensed them for your use in the following memorandum. Any portion not sufficiently clear, may be elucidated by a reference to the originals enclosed.

Mr. Anderton was a gentleman of good origin, closely connected with some of the first families in Yorkshire, where he had formed the acquaintance of Miss Bolton, while staying in the house of her great-aunt, Miss B——. He appears to have been of a most gentle and

* The late Miss Bolton.

amiable disposition, though unfortunately so shy and retiring as to have formed comparatively very few intimacies. All, however, who could be numbered among his acquaintance seem to have been equally astonished at the charge brought against him on the death of his wife, with whom he was always supposed, though from his retired habits little was positively known, to have lived upon terms of the most perfect felicity. As the event proved, the case would in effect never have come on for trial; but, had it done so, the defence would have brought forward overwhelming evidence of the incredibility of such a crime on the part of one of so gentle and affectionate a disposition.

During the four years and a half of their married life, there does not appear to have been a cloud upon their happiness. Mrs. Anderton's letters to her great-aunt, Miss B—— (to whom I am indebted for almost the whole of the important information I have been able to collect respecting the family) are full of expressions of attachment to her husband and instances of his devotion to her. Copies of several of these letters are enclosed and from these it will be seen how unvarying was their attachment to each other. Throughout the entire series, extending over the whole period of her married life, there is not a single expression which could lead to any other conclusion.

It is, however, evident that the delicate health with which Mrs. Anderton had been afflicted from her birth, still continued, and in two instances we have indications of the mysterious attacks noticed in the letter of Mrs. Vansittart, before quoted. These, however, appear to have been but very slight. They had for some years been of more and more rare occurrence, and from this date (October, 1852), we have no further record of anything of this kind. Still, Mrs. Anderton's general health continued very unsatisfactory, and almost everything seems to have been tried by her for its improvement. Among the enclosed correspondence are letters dated from Baden, Ems, Lucca, Cairo, and other places to which the Andertons had, at different times, gone for the health of one or other, Mr. Anderton being also, as stated in Mrs. Ward's letter of the 14th June, 1851,* extremely delicate.

Of this gentleman all accounts agree in stating that the chief ailment was a constitutional nervousness, mental as well as physical. The latter showed itself in the facility with which, though by no means deficient in courage, he could be startled by any sudden occurrence, however simple; the former, in his extreme sensitiveness to the opinions of those about him, and his dread of the slightest shadow of reproach on the name of which he was so justly proud. In the accompanying documents you will find instances of both these idiosyncrasies.

In the summer of 1854 Mr. Anderton's attention seems to have been drawn to the subject of Mesmerism. They had been spending some weeks at Malvern, where this science seems particularly in vogue, and had there made acquaintance with several of the patients at the different water-cure establishments, by some of whom Mr. Anderton

* Section I, No. 12.

was strongly urged to have recourse to mesmeric treatment both for Mrs. Anderton and himself.

The constant solicitations of these enthusiastic friends seem at length to have produced their effect, and the favourite operator of the neighbourhood was requested to try his skill on these new patients. On Mr. Anderton the only result seems to have been the inducing of such a state of irritation as might not unreasonably have been expected from so nervously excitable a temperament, in presence of the " manipulations " to which the votaries of mesmerism are subjected.   In the case of Mrs. Anderton, however, the result was, or was supposed to be, different.   Whether from some natural cause that, at the time, escaped attention, or whether solely from that force of imagination from which such surprising results are often found to arise, I cannot of course say ; but it is certain that some short time after the mesmeric " séances " had commenced, a decided though slight improvement was perceptible. This continued until the departure of the operator for Germany, which country he had only recently left on a short visit to England.

Notwithstanding the worse than failure in his own case, the certainly curious coincidence of his wife's recovery seems to have entirely imposed on Mr. Anderton, whose susceptibility of disposition appears indeed to have laid him especially open to the practices of quacks of every kind.Ⓐ So great was now his faith in this new remedy that he actually proposed to accompany the Professor to Germany rather than that his wife should lose the benefit of the accustomed " manipulations." He had proceeded to London, for the purpose of making the necessary preparations, when he was induced to pause by the remonstrances of several of his friends, who represented to him that a winter in the severe climate of Dresden—the place to which the Professor was bound—would probably be fatal to one of Mrs. Anderton's delicate constitution.

His medical adviser also, though himself professing belief in mesmerism, gave a similar opinion, while at the same time he obviated the difficulty respecting the mesmeric treatment of Mrs. Anderton, by offering an introduction to " one of the most powerful mesmerists in Europe," who had recently arrived in London, and who eventually proved to be the so-styled Baron R**.

This introduction appears to have finally decided Mr. Anderton against the Dresden expedition ; and, after a brief experience of his manipulations, Mrs. Anderton herself seems to have derived, in imagination at least, more benefit from them than even from those of her late attendant.   So thoroughly were they both impressed with the beneficial result of the Baron's " passes," etc., that Mr. Anderton, who had now resolved to settle in London for the autumn and winter, went so far as to take a ready-furnished house at Notting Hill, for the express purpose of having his new professor in his immediate neighbourhood. * Here the *séances* were continued often twice or three times a day, and though, of course, no one in his senses could really attribute such a result to the exercises of the Baron, it is certain that, from some cause or other, the health of Mrs. Anderton continued steadily to improve.

Matters had continued in this position for some weeks, when objections were raised by some of Mr. Anderton's relations to what they not unnaturally considered the very questionable propriety of the proceeding. There seems to have been a good deal of discussion on this point in which, however, Mr. Anderton's constitutional susceptibility finally carried the day against his newly-conceived predilections with respect to a practice so obviously calculated to expose him to unpleasant comment. The Baron, however, was not disposed so easily to relinquish a patient from whom he derived such large and regular profits. On being made acquainted with the decision respecting the cessation of his visits, he at once declared that his own direct manipulations were unnecessary, and that, if considered improper for one of the opposite sex, they could easily be made available at second-hand.

Having once swallowed the original imposition, any additional absurdity was of course easily disposed of, and it was now determined to avoid all occasion for offence ; Mrs. Anderton should henceforth be operated upon through the medium of a certain Mademoiselle Rosalie, a *clairvoyante* in the employment of the Baron, who, after being placed " *en rapport* " with the patient, was to convey to her the benefit of the manipulations to which she was herself subjected by the operator.

Into the precise *modus operandi* I need not now enter, but will only remark upon the fresh instance of the extraordinary powers of imagination displayed in the still more rapid improvement of Mrs. Anderton under this new form of treatment, and the marvellous " sympathy " so rapidly induced between her and the Baron's " medium."

Mademoiselle Rosalie was a brunette rather below the medium height, with slight but beautifully proportioned and active figure, sallow complexion, and dark hair and eyes. The only fault a *connoisseur* would probably find with her person would be the extreme breadth of her feet, though this might perhaps be accounted for by her former occupation, to be noticed later on. It is necessary for our purpose that this peculiarity should be kept in mind. In appearance she was at that time about thirty years old, but might very possibly have been younger, as the nature of her profession would probably entail a premature appearance of age. Altogether she formed a remarkable contrast to Mrs. Anderton, who was slight but tall, and fair, with remarkably small feet, and notwithstanding her ill-health, still looking a year or two less than her age. Between these very different persons, however, if we are to credit the enclosed letters, such a " sympathy " sprang up as would, on all ordinary hypotheses, be perfectly unaccountable. Mrs. Anderton could feel—or imagined that she felt—the approach of Mademoiselle Rosalie even before she entered the room; the mere touch of her hand seemed to afford immediate benefit, and within a very few weeks she became perfectly convalescent, and stronger than she had ever been before.

At this point I must again refer you to the depositions themselves, that of Mr. Morton, which here follows, being of too much importance to admit of condensation.

2—*Statement of Frederick Morton, Esq., late Lieutenant, R.A.*

My name is Frederick George Morton. In 1854, I was a lieutenant in the Royal Artillery, and was slightly wounded at the Battle of Inkerman, on the 5th of November of that year, the day after my arrival in the Crimea. It was before joining the battery to which I was appointed. I have since quitted the service, on the death of my father, and am now residing with my mother at Leeds. I was an old school friend of the late Mr. William Anderton, and knew him intimately for nearly fifteen years. I was present at his marriage with Miss Bolton, in August, 1851, and have since frequently visited at their house. During the time I was at Woolwich Academy, I spent every leave-out day with them, and frequently a good portion of the vacations. My father encouraged the intimacy, and I was as much at home in their house as in our own. My father was junior partner of one of the large manufacturing firms in Leeds. The Andertons generally lived in London, when they were not abroad; and on one occasion I went with them to Wiesbaden. I saw very little of them in 1854, as they were away the earlier part of the year, first at Ilfracombe, and then at Malvern, but I spent the 13th of October with them. I particularly remember the date, as I was on my way to the Crimea, where I was afterwards wounded, and the order had come very suddenly. When it came I had just gone to a friend's house for some pheasant-shooting, and I remember I was obliged to leave the second morning, and I spent the night at Anderton's, and embarked the next morning. I was to have gone for the first, but could not get away, and I lost the shooting altogether. It was on a Saturday that I embarked, because I remember we had church parade next day. That was the last time I saw Anderton. I was in Italy all that winter, with my wound and rheumatic fever; and in the summer of 1855 I was sent for to my father, who was ill for several months before he died, and after that I could not leave my mother. We only took in a weekly paper, and I did not hear of his having been taken up till three or four days after. I started to see him immediately, but was too late. It was not on account of any quarrel that we had not met. Quite the reverse. We were as good friends as ever to the last, and I would have given my life to serve him. I was on the most friendly terms with Mrs. Anderton. He was dotingly fond of her. I used to laugh, and say I was jealous of her, and they used to laugh too. I never saw two people so fond of one another. He was the best and kindest-hearted fellow I ever knew, only awfully nervous, and very sensitive about his family and his name. The only time we ever quarrelled was once at school, when I tried to chaff him by pretending to doubt something he had said ; it made him quite ill. He often said he would rather die than have any stain upon his name, which he was very proud of. On the day I speak of—13th October, 1854—I telegraphed to them at Notting Hill that I would dine and sleep there on my way out. I found Mrs. Anderton better than I had ever seen her before. She said it was all Baron R**'s doing, and that since Rosalie came she had got well faster than ever. She wanted to put off the Baron for that night, that we might have a quiet talk, but I would not let her ; and, besides, I wanted to see him and Rosalie. They came at about nine o'clock, and Mrs. Anderton lay on the sofa, and Rosalie sat on a chair by her side, and held her hand while the Baron sent her to sleep. It was Rosalie he put to sleep, not Mrs. Anderton. The latter did not go to sleep, but lay quite still on the sofa, while Anderton and I sat together at the farther end of the room, because he said we might " cross the mesmeric fluid." I don't know what he meant. Of course I know that it was all nonsense ; but I don't think Rosalie was shamming. I should go to sleep myself, if a man went on that way. When it was over, Mrs. Anderton said she felt much better, and I couldn't help laughing ; then Anderton sent her up to bed, and he and I and the Baron sat talking for an hour and more. I never saw Mrs. Anderton again, for I went away before she was up, but I used to hear of her from Anderton. What we talked of after she was gone was mesmerism. Of course I did not believe in it, and I said so ; and Anderton and the Baron tried to persuade me it was true. We were smoking, but Rosalie was there, and said she did not mind it. She always seemed to say whatever the Baron wanted, but I don't think she liked him. She did not join in the conversation. She said—or at least the Baron said—she could not speak English, but I am quite sure she must have understood it, or at all events a good deal. I have learned German, and sometimes I said something to her, and she answered ; and once I saw her look up so quickly when Anderton said something about " Julie," and the Baron said directly, in German, " not your Julie, child." I asked her, as she was going away, who Julie was, and she had just told me that she was her great friend, and a dancing girl, when the Baron gave her a look, and she stopped. That was as they were leaving. Before that, Rosalie was doing crochet, and we three were talking about mesmerism. They tried to make me believe it, and the Baron was telling all sorts of stories about a wonderful *clairvoyante*. That was his Julie, not Rosalie's. Of course I laughed at it all, and then they got talking about sympathies, and what a wonderful sympathy there was between twins, and the Baron told some more extraordinary stories. And when I wouldn't believe it, Anderton got quite vexed, and reminded me about the twin sister his wife had had, and who had been stolen by the gipsies. And then the Baron asked him about it, and he told him the

whole story, only making him promise not to tell it again, because they
were afraid of her being reminded of it, and that was why it was never
spoken of. The Baron seemed quite interested, and drew his chair
close in between us. We were speaking low, that Rosalie might not
hear. I remember the Baron said it was so curious he must take a
note of it, and he wrote it all down in his pocket-book. He took down
the dates, and all about it. He was very particular about the dates.
I am sure Rosalie could have heard nothing of all this ; not even if she
had understood English. We had gone to the window, and were too
far off. Besides, we spoke low. Afterwards the Baron seemed thought-
ful, and did not speak for some time. Anderton and I got to mesmerism again, and he got a number of some magazine—the ' Ziost,'
or something of that sort—to prove me something. He read me some
wonderful story about eating by deputy, and when I would not believe
it, he called the Baron, and asked if it was not true, and he said perfectly, he had known it himself. He started when Anderton spoke to
him, as if he had been thinking of something else, and he had to repeat
it again. I know it was something about eating by deputy, because
afterwards, when I was wounded and had the fever, I used to think of
it and wish I could take physic that way. You will find it in the
" Zoist " for that month—October, 1854.* I remember saying at the
time, that it was lucky for the young woman that the fellow didn't eat
anything unwholesome, and Anderton laughed at it. The Baron did
not laugh. He stood for ever so long without saying a word, and
looking quite odd. I thought that I had offended him by laughing.
Anderton spoke to him, and he jumped again, and I saw this time he
had let his cigar out. I remember that, because he tried to light it
again by mine, and his hand shook so he put mine out instead. He
said he was cold, and shut the window. He would not have another
cigar, but said he must go away, it was late. Anderton and I sat
smoking for some time. I tried to persuade him to give up mesmerism,
and he said Mrs. Anderton was so well now, he thought she could do
without it, and that she would give it up in a few weeks. I heard from
him afterwards, in November, that the Baron had left town for some
weeks. When I was ill at Scutari, after my wound, I wrote to ask him
to meet me at Naples, and he started with Mrs. Anderton in December,
but was stopped at Dover by Mrs. Anderton's illness. I have had
several letters from him since, and am quite ready to give copies of
them ; all but the bits that are private. I have read over this statement, and it is all quite true. I am quite ready to swear to it in a court
of justice, if required. I wish to add, that I am quite certain poor
Anderton had nothing to do with his poor wife's death. I will swear
to that.

* An extract from the magazine here quoted will be given later on in the case.

3—*Statement of Julie.**

Manchester, 3 Aug., 1857.

" Dear Sir,

In compliance with your instructions of the 11th ult., I forward deposition of Julia Clark, *alias* Julie, *alias* Miss Montgomery, &c., at present of the Theatre Royal, duly attested.

Dear Sir,

Yours faithfully,

WILLIAM SMITH."

" I am a dancer, and my name is Julia Clark : I have performed under the name of Julie, and other names. I am at present called Miss Montgomery. I knew the girl called Rosalie. We were for several years together in Signor Leopoldo's company. I forget how many. She did the tight-rope business, and had ten shillings a week and her keep. In our company she was called ' The Little Wonder.' Her real name was Charlotte Brown. She was about ten years old when I joined the company. I do not know her history. She did not know it herself. She often told me so. She would have told me if she did. She passed as the niece of old Mrs. Brown. Mrs. Brown was the money-taker. She took Lotty's money and found her in clothes. Lotty is Rosalie. Some of our ladies said she had been bought from a tramp. Of course I did not believe it. They said it out of spite. Lotty did the tight-rope business for about five years after I knew her. She was a beautiful figure, only her feet were very broad.† All tight-rope dancers are. The rope spreads them. Otherwise her figure was perfect. She was nervous. Not very, but rather. She used to tremble before she went on. It was not from fear. She was ill sometimes. Not often. Sometimes she caught cold from sitting on the damp ground to undress when she was hot with dancing. She got stronger as she grew up. Sometimes she felt ill, and did not know why. She had bad headaches. When she was in that way, physic was no good, only brandy. Brandy took away the headaches. She used to drink brandy sometimes, but not like some of our ladies. I never saw her the worse for liquor. Her headaches were not from drinking. Certainly not. They came and went away again. Brandy took them away. I only know of once that she has been ill since she left the company. She wrote and told me of it. I have the letter still. It is not dated, but there was an extract from a newspaper in it about her which is date some time in October, 1852.‡ The day of the month is cut off. She gave up the tight-rope business because of a fall. That was from being nervous. She was not drunk. She had not been drinking. A glass drop fell from the chandelier and frightened her. That was all.

---

* The difficulty of tracing this witness, from the slight clue afforded by Mr. Morton's statement, occasioned considerable delay.

† Section II, No. 1.

‡ Section II, No. 1.

She was very much hurt. One foot was sprained, and the doctors at the hospital said she must never go on the wire again. She was two months there. When she came out the circus was shut up. The company was all dispersed except her and me and Mr. Rogers, and the gentleman who did the comic business. Mr. Rogers was Signor Leopoldo. He took a music-hall. I think it was in Liverpool. He got another singing lady and gentleman, and we gave entertainments. Every evening Mr. Rogers gave a short lecture on mesmerism, and Lotty was his subject. She was very clever at that. Of course she was not really asleep. One night she stopped in the middle. The manager was very angry. She tried to go on, but she fainted, and had to be carried off. She said some gentleman in the stalls had done it. Next morning the gentleman called and took her away. He gave the Signor £50. He was the Baron R**. I knew it from Lotty. She has written to me several times. These are her letters. They are rubbed at the edges. It is from keeping them in my pocket. I do not think she ever left the Baron, but I do not know. The last letter I ever had from her was from his house. It was in the first week of November, 1854. I got it in Plymouth. It was the only week I was there before I went to Dublin for the pantomime. She said she was going to be married, but must not tell me who to just yet. I never heard from her since. I have written several times, but my letters have been returned. I have no idea who she married. It could not have been the Baron. She disliked him too much. She stayed with him because he paid her well. Partly that, and partly because she said she couldn't help doing what he told her. She said he really did mesmerise her, and that she could see in her sleep. She did not live with the Baron as his wife. Only as his medium. If she had she would have told me. I am quite sure she would. I am quite certain there was never any connection between her and the Baron except what I have said. Of course I cannot swear she did not marry him, but I should think it very unlikely. Why should she when she disliked him so much ? All this is true. I believe Signor Leopoldo is now somewhere abroad.

(signed) JULIA CLARK, alias JULIE."

(Read over to the deponent and signed by her in the presence of William Burton, J.P.
August 2nd, 1857.

4—*Statement of Leopoldo.*

N.B. This statement was obtained with some difficulty, and only on an express promise of immunity from any legal proceeding, in respect of the deponent's relations with the girl Rosalie, *alias* Angelina Fitz Eustace, *alias* the " Little Wonder," *alias* Charlotte Brown. The statement was enclosed in the following note :

" Signor Leopoldo, tragedian, &c., &c., &c., presents his compliments to R. Henderson, Esq., and in consideration of the assurance that 'what is done cannot now be amended,' I have the honour to forward the required information, in confidence that you will not keep the word of promise to the ear and break it to the hope, and thus ' my simple truth shall be abused.'

Sir, your most humble servant,
(signed) THOMAS ROGERS."

Deposition of Signor Leopoldo, Tragedian ; Professor of Fencing and Elocution ; Equestrian, Gymnastic, and Funambulistic Artiste ; Sole Proprietor and Manager of the Great Olympian Circus, &c., &c., &c.

" I, Signor Leopoldo, tragedian, &c., &c., &c., do hereby depose and declare that the girl, Charlotte Brown, commonly known as the celebrated ' Little Wonder,' was transferred by me to my celebrated Olympian Company in the month of July, 1837, at Lewes, in the County of Sussex, where the celebrated Olympian Circus was at that time performing with great success and crowded houses. And this deponent further maketh oath and saith that I, the said Signor Leopoldo, tragedian, &c., &c., &c., did in consideration of the services of the said Charlotte Brown, commonly known as the celebrated ' Little Wonder,' pay to a certain person or persons claiming to be the parent or parents of the said Charlotte Brown, commonly known as the celebrated ' Little Wonder,' the sum of five pounds (£5), which person or persons were of the tribe or tribes commonly known as gipsies or Egyptians. And this deponent furthermore maketh oath and saith that I, Signor Leopoldo, tragedian, &c., &c., &c., cannot tell whether the said Charlotte Brown, commonly known as the ' Little Wonder,' was really the child of the person or persons, gipsy or gipsies, aforesaid, or that her name was Charlotte Brown, or any other of the hereinbefore stated and deposed, but only that her linen was marked C.B. which initials do set forth and represent the name of Charlotte Brown.

Witness our hand and seal this 4th day of January, in the year of grace, one thousand eight hundred and fifty-eight.

(Signed) THOMAS ROGERS."

5—Statement of Edward Morris, Clerk in the Will Office, Doctors' Commons.

My name is Edward Morris. I am a clerk in the Will Office at Doctors' Commons, and my duty is to assist those who wish to search wills deposited in our office. On the 14th October, 1854, Baron R** came to the office and searched in several wills. One was the will of a Mr. Wilson, copy of which is herewith enclosed. I remember this will particularly, because I had an altercation with the Baron respecting his wish to copy parts of it. He wished to make extracts, and I told him it was not allowed ; only the dates and the names of the executors. He persisted, and I said I must report it. He then laughed, and said it did not matter, and he tapped his forehead, and said he could make a note of it there. He read parts of the will over two or three times and gave it back to me. He then said, " You shall see, my friend," and laughed again, and he made me follow him while he repeated several pages of the will by rote. He laughed again when he had done, and asked if he might copy it now. I said no ; and he laughed again, and wrote for some time in his pocket-book, looking up at me every now and then and laughing. I was angry, partly because he laughed, and partly because he kept me there when I wanted to get away. I had leave for a week to go to the Isle of Wight and see my aunt. I wanted to get there that night because the next day was my birthday. He made me miss the train, and as the next day was Sunday, I did not get there till late. That is how I remember the date. I am sure of the year because my aunt only went to the Isle of Wight the November previously, and died in the spring of 1855. I am quite sure it was the Baron. I should recognise him anywhere. He is a short, stout man, with a rather florid complexion and reddish hair, rather light. He has large fat hands, white and well-kept, and an immense head. He dresses all in black, and wears large spectacles of light blue. I don't think it is because his eyes are weak. I am sure it is not ; for when he takes off his spectacles, I never saw such extraordinary eyes. I can't describe them, only that they are very large and bright. I never could look at them long enough to make out the colour, but they are very dark, I think black, and they put one out to look at them, otherwise there is nothing very remarkable about him. I recognised him that day from having seen him before at a mesmeric lecture, when I asked his name.

6—*Memorandum by Mr. Henderson.*

I enclose the will, of which the following is an abstract :

" Mr. Wilson, of the firm of Price and Wilson, Calcutta, who died in 1825, leaves the sum of £25,375, three per cent. consols, to his niece, Gertrude Wilson (afterwards Lady Bolton), and to her children, if any, or their heirs in regular succession, whether male or female. In default of any such heirs, the money to be made over to trustees selected by the Governor General of India for the time being, from among the leading merchants of Calcutta, for the purpose of founding, under certain restrictions, an institution among the hills for the children of those who could not afford to send them home to England."

The will also provides that should any female taking under it die during her coverture, the husband shall retain a life interest in the property.

SECTION III

1—*Extracts from Mrs. Anderton's Journal.*

Aug. 13, 1854. Here we are, then, finally established at Notting Hill. Jane laughs at us for coming to town just as everyone else is leaving it, but in my eyes, and I am sure in dear William's too, that is the pleasantest time for us. Poor Willie, he grows more and more sensitive to blame from any one, and has been sadly worried by this discussion about our Dresden trip. The new professor to-morrow. I wonder what he will be like.

Aug. 14. And so *that* is the new Professor ! I do not think I was ever so astonished in my life. That little stout squat man, the most powerful mesmerist in Europe ! And yet he certainly is powerful, for he had scarcely made a pass over me before I felt a glow through my whole frame. There is something about him, too, when one comes to look at him more closely, which puzzles me very much. He is certainly not the commonplace man he appears, though it would be difficult just now to say what makes me so sure of it.

Aug. 25. Quite satisfied now. How could I have ever thought the Baron commonplace ! And yet, at first sight, his appearance is certainly against him. He is not a man with whom I should like to quarrel. I don't think he would have much compunction in killing any one who offended him, or who stood in his way. How quietly he talks of those horrid experiments in the medical schools, and the tortures they inflict on the poor hospital patients. Willie says it is all nonsense, and say all doctors talk so ; but I can't help feeling that there is something different about him. And yet he is certainly doing me good.

*Sept.*1. Better and better, and yet I cannot conquer the strange feeling which is growing upon me about the Baron. He is certainly an extraordinary man. What a grasp he takes of anything on which he rests his hand even for a moment ; and how perfectly he seems to disregard anything that stands in his way. This morning I was at the window when he came, and I was quite frightened when I saw him, as I thought, so nearly run over. But I might have spared my anxiety, for my gentleman just walked quietly on, while the poor horse started almost across the road. Had it caught sight of those wonderful green eyes of his, that it seemed so frightened ? What eyes they are ! You can hardly ever see them ; but when you do !—And yet the man is certainly doing me good.

Sept. 11. So it is settled that the Baron is not to mesmerise me himself any more. Am I sorry or glad ? At all events, I hope they will not now worry poor William. . . .

Sept. 13. First day of Mademoiselle Rosalie. Seems a nice person enough ; but it feels very odd to lie there on the sofa while someone else is being mesmerised for one.

Sept. 15. This new plan is beginning to answer. I think I feel the mesmerism even more than when I was mesmerised myself, and this way one gets all the pleasures and none of the disagreeables. It *is* so delicious. Looked back to-day at my Malvern journals. So odd to see how I disliked the idea at first, and now I could hardly live without it.

Sept. 29. I think we shall soon be able to do without the Baron

altogether. I am sure Rosalie and I could manage very well by ourselves. What a wonderful thing this mesmerism is ! To think that
the mere touch of another person's hand should soothe away pain, and
fill one with health and strength. Really, if I had not always kept a
journal, I should feel bound to keep one now, as a record of the wonderful effects of this extraordinary cure. Got up this morning with a
nasty headache. Eyes heavy and pulse low. Poor William in
terrible tribulation, when lo ! in comes little Mademoiselle Rosalie
and the Baron. The gentleman makes a pass or two—the lady pops
her little, dry, monkey-looking paw upon my forehead, and *presto !*
the headache has vanished, and I'm calling for chocolate and toast !
Sept. 30. A blank day. Headache again this morning, and looking
out anxiously for my little brown " good angel," when in comes the
Baron, with the news that she cannot come. Up all night with a dying
lady, and so fagged this morning that he is afraid she would do me
more harm than good. I am sure she cannot feel more fagged than I
do, poor girl. But, after all, in spite of the delight of doing so much
good, what a life it must be !
Oct. 1. Rosalie here again. Headache vanished. Everything bright
as the October sun outside. I am getting quite fond of that girl.
How I wish she could speak something besides German. . . .
Oct. 4. It is quite extraordinary what a hold that poor girl, Rosalie, is
taking upon me. I am even beginning to dream of her at night. . . .
Oct. 6. Headache again this morning, and a message that Rosalie
cannot come. How provoking that it is on the same day. . . .
Oct. 12. I think I shall really soon begin to know when poor Rosalie
has been overworked. Headache again to-day, and I had a presenti-
ment that she would not be able to come. . . .
Oct. 20.* So now the Baron is going to leave us. Well, I am indeed
thankful that he can now be so well spared. Jane Morgan here to-day,
and of course laughing at the idea of mesmerism doing any good.
She could not deny, though, how wonderfully better I am, and indeed,
but for those tiresome headaches, which always seem to come just
when poor Rosalie is too tired to take them away, I am really quite well
and strong.
Oct. 31. Something evidently wrong between poor Rosalie and the
Baron. She has evidently been crying, and I suppose it must be from
sympathy, but I feel exactly as if I had been crying too. Very little
satisfaction from the mesmerism to-day. It seems rather as if it had
given me some of poor Rosalie's depression. How I wish she could
speak English, or that I could speak German, and then I would find out
what is the matter. Perhaps she is to lose her work when the Baron
goes. Mem : to ask him to-morrow.
Nov. 1. ' No. He says he shall certainly take her with him to Germany,
and " he hopes that that will have a beneficial effect." What can he
mean ? He says she is quite well, but throws out mysterious

* Compare Section II, 2 & 5.

insinuations as to something being wrong with her. How I do wish
I could speak German.

Nov. 3. Still that uncomfortableness between the Baron and Rosalie.
I am sure there is something wrong, and that she wants to speak to me
about it, but is afraid of him. It certainly is strange that he should
never leave us alone. Mem : to ask William to get him out of the way
for a little while to-morrow, though what good that will be when she
and I cannot understand each other, I hardly know after all. . . .

Nov. 4. What a day this has been ! I feel quite tired out with the
excitement, and yet I cannot make up my mind to go to bed until I
have written it all down. In the first place, this is to be my last visit
from Rosalie, at all events till they come back from the continent. I
cannot help perceiving that William is not altogether sorry that she is
going. Dear fellow ! I do really believe that he is more than half
jealous of my extraordinary feeling for her. And certainly it is
extraordinary that a woman quite in another class of life, of whom one
knows nothing, should have taken such a hold upon one. I suppose
it must be the mesmerism, which certainly is a very mysterious thing.
If it is so, it is at all events very fortunate it did not take that turn
with the Baron himself. Ugh ! I can really begin to understand now
all the objections I thought so foolish and so tiresome three or four
months ago, before Rosalie first came. And yet, after all, I don't
think—in spite of mesmerism or anything else—one need ever have
been afraid of liking the Baron too much. I could quite understand
being afraid of him. Rosalie evidently is, and to own the truth so am
I a little, or I should not have been beaten in that way to-day. To-day
was my last *séance* with Rosalie, and I had made up my mind to get
the Baron out of the way, and try and get something out of Rosalie.
They came at two o'clock as usual, and as I thought I would not lose a
chance, I had got dear William to lie in wait in his study, and call to the
Baron as he passed, in hopes that Rosalie would come up alone. That
was no use, however, for the Baron kept his stout little self perseveringly between her and the staircase, and when I went—thinking to be
very clever—to the top of the staircase and called to her to come up, it
only gave him an excuse for breaking away from poor William altogether,
and coming straight up to me before her. I *was* so provoked, I could
hardly be civil. Well, of course, the Baron was in a great hurry, and
we went to work at once with the mesmerising. When that was done,
we both tried to keep them talking, and I made signs to William to
get the Baron out of the way. I was really beginning to get quite
anxious about it, and kept on repeating over and over to myself the two
German words I had learned on purpose from Jane Morgan this
morning. It was no use, however, and I began to grow quite nervous ;
and I am quite sure Rosalie saw what I was wanting, for she seemed
to get fidgety too, and then that made me more nervous still. At last
the Baron declared he must go, and they both got up to leave. William
would have given it up, but he says I looked so imploringly at him he

could not resist, so made one more effort by asking the Baron to come to his study for a short private consultation. This he refused, saying he had not the time, but could say anything needful where we were. Then William told me to take Rosalie into the next room, but the Baron would not have that either, thought he laughed when he said he could not trust to a lady's punctuality in this case, but if I would leave Rosalie she would not understand anything that was said. Of course this would not do, and at last William, with more presence of mind and determination that I should have thought him capable of, took him by the button-hole and fairly drew him away into the further window, where he began whispering eagerly to him to draw off his attention. I suppose it was the consciousness of a sort of strategem, but my heart beat quite fast as I brought out my two words, " Gibst' was ? " and I could see that hers was so too. She seemed surprised at my speaking to her in German, and certainly I was no less so to hear her answer in English, with a slight accent certainly, but still in quite plain English—" Don't seem to listen. I am . . ." and then she stopped suddenly and turned quite pale, and I could feel all my own blood rush back to my heart with such a throb! I looked up, and there were the Baron's eyes fixed upon us. Poor Rosalie seemed quite frightened, and I declare I felt so too. At all events, we neither of us ventured on another word, and the next minute the Baron succeeded in fairly shaking off poor William and taking his leave. So there is an end of my little romance about Rosalie. I am *sure* there is something in it. Why, if she had nothing particular to say, should she have taken the trouble of learning that little bit of English ? and why—but I must not sit here all night speculating about this, which after all is, I dare-say, nothing at all. It is positively just twelve o'clock.

Nov. 6. How strange! There is certainly some mystery about Rosalie and the Baron. I am quite certain I saw them in a cab to-gether this morning, and yet they were to cross on Saturday night and be in Paris yesterday. I wonder whether they were late after all, and yet an hour and a half is surely time enough to London Bridge, and if he had missed the train I should think he would have come to us yesterday. At all events he might have gone early this morning. It is very odd. . . .

Nov. 7. I wonder whether anyone ever had such a husband as I have got. Yesterday he must needs worry himself with the idea that I am fretting about the loss of my mesmerism—as if I could possibly think a moment about the loss of anything when I had got him with me. So nothing would satisfy him but that we must go to the Haymarket to see " Paul Pry " and the Spanish Dancers. I have not laughed so much for many a long day. I don't like all that violent dancing, so we came away directly after the absurd little farce—" How to Pay the Rent." How we did laugh at it, to be sure, and the absurdities of that little monkey, Clark. Wright, too, in " Paul Pry," is quite inimit-able. Dear William, how good it was of him ! . . .

Dec. 5. Just going to the theatre again when news came of poor Harry Morton's illness. My own dear William, how good he is to everyone. And so prompt, too. Touch his heart or his honour, and the Duke himself could not be more quick or decided. The news only came as we were dressing, and to-morrow we are off to Naples to meet poor Mr. Morton and nurse him.

Dec. 6. There is no one like Willie. After all the scramble we have had to get ready, he would not take me across when it was so rough. So we have taken two dear little rooms, from day to day, because Willie cannot bear the publicity of a hotel, and I am sure I hate it too, and we are to wait till it if fine enough to cross.

Dec. 9. Still here; but the wind has gone down almost suddenly within the last three hours, and to-morrow morning I hope we really shall cross. Dear William getting quite worried; I persuaded him to take me to a lecture that was going on, and while we were there the wind went down, and we have been packing up ever since. Twelve o'clock! and William calling to me. I *must* just put down about Mr. . . . . Good Heaven! What is the matter? I feel so ill—quite——

2—*Statement of Dr. Watson.*

My name is James Watson, and I am a physician of about thirty years' standing. In 1854, I was practising at Dover. On the night of the 9th of December in that year I was sent for hurriedly to see a lady, of the name of Anderton, who had been taken suddenly ill immediately after her return from a lecture at the Town Hall, which she had attended with her husband. The message was brought by the servant from the lodgings where they were living. On our way to the house she told me that " the lady was dying, and the gentleman quite distracted." On arriving at the house I found Mr. Anderton supporting his wife in his arms. He seemed greatly agitated, and cried, " For God's sake be quick—I think she has got the cholera ! " Mrs. Anderton was on the couch in her dressing-room, partially undressed, but with two or three blankets thrown over her, as she seemed shivering with the cold. There was a good fire in the room, but notwithstanding this and the blankets her hands and feet were both quite chilly.* I asked Mr. Anderton why she had not been got to bed, to which he replied, that she had been vomiting, until within a very few moments, so violently, that they had been unable to move her. Almost immediately on my arrival the vomiting recommenced, though there appeared to be now hardly anything left in the stomach to come away. The retching continued with unabated violence for more than an hour after the stomach had been evidently completely emptied,

---

* This portion of Dr. Watson's statement, relating entirely to the symptoms of Mrs. Anderton's case, though some details are excluded, necessarily contains much that must be interesting only to the medical profession and disagreeable to the general reader. The following paragraph may therefore be passed over, merely noting that the symptoms were such as would be compatible with antimonial poisoning.

and was accompanied with great purging and severe cramps both in the stomach and in the extremities. I at once sent to my house for a portable bath I happened to have hired for my own wife's use, and, on its arrival, placed Mrs. Anderton in it at a temperature of 98°, having previously added ¾lb. of mustard. While waiting for the bath, I administered thirty drops of laudanum in a wineglassful of hot brandy-and-water, but without, in any degree, checking the purging, which continued almost incessantly, and was of a most watery character. It was accompanied also by violent pains and great swelling of the *epigastrium*. A fresh dose of opium was equally unsuccessful, nor was any amelioration of symptoms produced by the exhibition of prussian acid and creosote. On removing the patient from the warm bath, It had her carefully placed in bed, shortly after which she began to perspire profusely, but without any relief to the other symptoms. . . . I now began to fear that some deleterious substance had been un-consciously swallowed, the more especially as the patient had, up to the very moment of her seizure, been in unusually good health. I there-fore made careful examinations, with the view to detecting the presence of arsenic ; and instituted, by the aid of Mr. Anderton, the strictest inquiries as to whether there was in the house any preparation con-taining this or any other irritant poison. Nothing of the kind could, however, be found, nor were such tests, as I was at the time in a position to apply, able to detect anything of the kind to which my suspicions were directed. Deliberate poisoning proved, moreover, on consideration, entirely out of the question, as there could be no question of Mr. Anderton's devoted attachment to his wife, and the people of the house were entire strangers to her. Moreover, the length of time since any food had been taken was almost conclusive against any such a supposition. Mrs. Anderton had dined at six o'clock, and between that hour and midnight, when the attack came on, had eaten nothing but a biscuit and part of a glass of sherry-and-water, the remainder of which was in the glass upon the dressing-table when I arrived. Since then I have removed portions of all the matters tested, as well as the remaining wine-and-water, and have had them thoroughly examined by a scientific chemist, but equally without result. I am compelled, therefore, to believe that the symptoms arose from some natural though undiscovered cause. Possibly from a sudden chill in coming from the heated rooms into the night air, though this seems hardly compatible with the fact that she never complained of cold during the long drive home, and that she was seated comfortably in her dressing-room, making her customary entries in her journal, when the attack came on. Another very suspicious circumstance was that, afterwards mentioned by her, of a strong metallic taste in the mouth, a symptom sometimes occasioned, and in conjunction likewise with the others noticed in her case, by the exhibition of excessive doses of antimony in the form of emetic tartar. This medicine, however, had never been prescribed for her, nor was there any possibility of her having had access to any in mistake. At Mr. Anderton's request, however, I exhibited the remedies used in such a case, as port wine, infusion of oak-bark, &c., but with as little effect as the other medicines. Indeed, the remedies of whatever kind were precluded from exercising their full action by the extreme irritability of the stomach, by which they were ejected almost as soon as swallowed. This being the case, I abandoned any further attempt at the exhibition of the heavy doses I had hitherto employed, or indeed of drugs of any kind, and confined myself, until the irritation of the *epigastrium* should have been in some measure allayed, to a treatment I have occasionally found successful in somewhat similar cases ; the administration, that is to say, of simple soda-water in repeated doses of a teaspoonful at a time. I have often found this to remain with good effect upon the stomach when everything else was at once rejected, nor was I disappointed in the present case. About an hour after commencing this treatment, the first violence of the symptoms began to subside, and by the next afternoon the case had resolved itself into an ordinary one of severe *gastro-enteritis*, which I then proceeded to treat in the ordinary manner. After quite as short a period as I could possibly have expected, this also was subdued, leaving the patient, however, in a state of great prostration, and subject to night-perspirations of a most lowering character. I now began to throw in tonics, and to resort, though very cautiously, to more invigorating diet. Under this treatment she continued steadily to improve, though the perspirations still continued, and her constitution cannot be said to have at all recovered the severe shock it had sustained by the month of April, 1855, when they left Dover, by my recommendation, for change of air. Since that time I have not seen her. I am quite unable to account for the seizure from any cause but that of a chill, an hypothesis which, I must admit, rests its authority almost entirely on the fact that no other can be found.

3—*Extracts from Mrs. Anderton's Journal.—Continued.*

Jan. 20, 1855. At last I get back once more to my old brown friend.* Dear old thing, how pleasant its old face seems ! Very little to-day, though ; only a word or two, just to say it is done. Oh, how it tries one !

Jan. 25. My own dear husband's birthday ; and, thank Heaven ! I am once more able to sit with him. Oh ! how kind he had been through all these weary weeks, when I have been so fretful and impatient. Why should suffering make one cross ? God knows, I *have* suffered. I never thought to live through that terrible night. It makes me shudder to think of it. And then, that horrid, deathlike, leaden taste—that was worst of all. Well, thank God, I am better now, but *so* weak. I am quite tired with writing even these few lines.

Feb. 12. How weak I still am ! Walked out to-day with dear William for the first time upon the pier, but had scarcely got to the end of it

* Apparently the journal, which is bound in brown Russian leather.

when I felt so tired I was obliged to sit down, while poor William
went to fetch a chair to take me home.

Feb. 13. I have been quite startled to-day. I was talking to Dr.
Watson about my being so tired yesterday, and about how very weak
I still was, and how ill I had been—and, at last, he let slip that, at the
time, he thought I had been poisoned. It gave me quite a turn, and
then he tried to make me talk of something else, but I could not get it
out of my head, and kept coming back and back to it, and wondering
who could have had any possible interest in poisoning poor me. And
so we went on talking ; and, at last, Dr. Watson said something which
let out that at first he had suspected—William ! my own William ! my
precious, precious husband ! Oh ! I thought I should have choked
on the spot. I don't know what I said, but I do know I could not have
said too much, and poor William tried to laugh it off, and said : " Who
else would have gained anything by it ? Would he not have had that
miserable £25,000 ? and besides him, there was no one but the
Charities in India, and they could not have done it, because they would
not exist till we were gone ; " but I could see how he winced at the
idea, and I felt as though my blood were really boiling in my veins.
And then that man—oh ! how thankful I shall be when we can get
away from him !—tried to persuade me that he had not really thought
it, I should think not, indeed ! and that he soon saw it was impossible, and all that ; and at last, I fairly burst out crying with passion,
and ran out of the room. And—and—I could cry now to think of my
poor dear Willie being—and I shall, too, if I go on thinking about it
any longer, so I will write no more to-night.

Feb. 15. No journal yesterday, I really could not trust myself to write.
And poor Willie, though he tried to laugh at it, I could see how bitterly
he felt the imputation. Good Heavens ! think if that wretched man
had really charged him with it. It would have killed him. I know
it would, and he would rather have died a thousand times. Well, I
must not think of it any more. Only, once more, thank Heaven ! we
shall soon be going away.

April 7. Back once more at home, thank Heaven ! But how slow,
how very slow this convalescence, as they call it, is. Oh ! shall I
ever be well again, as I was last year before that horrid day at Dover !

May 3. So we are to leave England for a time, and try the German
baths. I am almost thankful for it. I have grown very fond, too, of
this dear little luxurious house, though I could hardly say why. It is
like my wonderful fancy for Rosalie. Ah, poor Rosalie ! I wonder
where she is now, and when they will return. I cannot help thinking
she might do me some good. But, as I was saying ; fond as I am of
this dear little house, I shall be really glad to leave it for a time, and see
what change of air will do for me. If I could only get rid of those
terrible night perspirations. It is they that pull me down so, and make
me so weak and miserable. Oh ! what would I not give to be well
once more, if it were only to get rid of the memory of that time.

July 7. Safe at Baden Baden ; and too early as yet for the majority of the English pleasure-seekers. What a delicious place it is ; I declare I quite feel myself better already. . . .

Sept. 11. Really almost well again. Quite a comfortable talk to-day with dear Willie about that foolish Dr. Watson ; the first time the subject has been mentioned between us, since that day when I got into such a passion about it. Poor man, he was hardly worth going into such a rage about. We heard to-day of his having made some terrible blunder in the new place he has gone to, and lost all his practice by killing some poor old woman through it. It was this made us talk of his poisoning notion, and oh ! how glad I was to see that dear Willie had quite got over his nervousness about it. We had quite along talk ; and, at last, he promised me faithfully never to say a word more about it to anyone.

Oct. 10. Home again at last, and in our own dear little house. And really I feel as well and strong as this time last year. Dear William, too, how happy he is ; the shadow seems quite to have passed away. God grant it may not return.

Oct. 30. An eventful day. All the morning at the Crystal Palace, and just as we returned who should walk in but the Baron R**! It was just a year since he left us, but he had not altered in the very least. I do not think that short, square figure, with the impenetrable rosy face, and the large white hands, and those wonderful great green eyes that you can so rarely catch, and when you have caught, so invariably wish you had let alone, can ever change. I am afraid I was not very cordial to him. I ought to be, for he has done great things for me ; and yet somehow, when I saw him, I felt quite a cold shudder run all through me. Dear William saw it, and asked if I were ill, and when I laughed, and " No, it was only someone walking over my grave," I could not help fancying that for a moment the Baron's lips seemed to turn quite white, and I just caught one glance from those awful eyes that seemed as if it would read me through and through. And yet after all it may have only fancy, for the next moment he was talking in his rich, quiet voice as though nothing could ever disturb him. So Rosalie is gone. That is clear at all events, though what has exactly become of her I cannot quite so well understand. From all I can make out, she seems, poor girl, to have married very foolishly, and it was that that was the matter between them when they went away last year. The Baron seemed indeed to hint at something even worse, but he would not speak out plainly, and I would defy anyone to make that man say one word more than he may choose. Poor Rosalie, I hope she has not come to any harm.

Nov. 1. Another visit from the Baron, to say good-bye before his return to—his wife ! How strange we should never have heard of her, and even now I cannot make out whether he has married since he left us or whether he was always so. Certainly that man is a mystery, and just now it pleases him to talk especially in enigmas. He does not seem disposed, however, to put up with vague information on our part. I thought he would never have done questioning poor William about me and my illness, and at last he drew it out of me—not out of William, dear fellow—what that foolish Dr. Watson had said. After all, I am not sorry I told him, for it was quite a relief to hear him speak so strongly of the absurdity of such an idea, and I am sure it was a comfort to poor William. He—the Baron—spoke very strongly too about the danger of setting such ideas about, and particularly cautioned dear Willie not to mention it to anyone. I knew he would not have done so any way, but this will make him more comfortable.

April 3. Such a delightful day, and so tired. I never saw Richmond look so lovely, and how dear Willie and I did enjoy ourselves in that lovely park. But oh ! I am so sleepy. Not a word more.

April 5. Another lovely day—strolling about Lord Holland's Park all the morning, and this evening some music in our own dear little drawing-room. How happy—how very happy—good Heaven, what is this ? That old horrible leaden taste—and oh, so deadly sick. . . .

April 6. Thank Heaven the attack seems to have passed away. Oh, how it frightened me. Thank Heaven, too, I was able to keep the worst from dear William, and he did not know how like it was to that other dreadful time.

April 20. Again that horrible sickness, and worse—oh, far worse— still, that awful deadly leaden taste. Worse this time, too, than the last. In bed all day yesterday. Poor Willie terribly anxious. Pray Heaven it may not come again.

May 6. Another attack, God help me ! if this should go on, I do not know what will become of me. Already I am beginning to feel weaker and weaker. Poor Willie !—these last three days have been terrible ones for him. However, the doctor says it will pass off. Pray Heaven it may !

May 25. More sickness, more derangement, more of that horrible leaden taste. The doctor himself is beginning to look uncomfortable, and I can see that poor Willie's mind is reverting to that terrible sugges-tion a year ago. Thank Heaven I have as yet managed to conceal from him and from Dr. Dodsworth that horrid deadly taste which made such an impression on Dr. Watson. Oh, when will this end !

June 10. A horrible suspicion is taking possession of me. What can this mean ? I look back through my journal, and it is every fort-night that this fearful attack returns. The 5th and 18th of April— 3rd and 21st of May—and now again the 7th of this month. And that terrible leaden taste which is now almost constantly in my mouth ; and with every attack my strength failing—failing—O God, what can it be ?

June 26. Another fortnight—another attack. There *must* be foul play somewhere. And yet who could—who would do such a thing ? Thank Heaven I have still concealed from my poor William that worst symptom of all, the horrible leaden taste which is now never out of my

mouth. My precious Willie, how kind, how good he is to me. . . .
July 12. I cannot hold out much longer now. Each time the attack
returns I lose something of the little, the very little strength that is left.
God help me, I feel now that I must go. . . . The Baron came to-
day, and for a moment my poor boy's face lighted up with hope again.
They had a long discussion before the doctor would consent to consult
with him, but after that, they seemed to change the medicines. But
something must have gone wrong, for I have never seen Dr. Dodsworth
look so grave.
Aug. 1. I think the end is drawing very near now. This last attack
has weakened me more than ever, and I write this in my bed. I
shall never rise from it again. My poor, poor Willie. . . . Three days
I have been in bed now, but I have taken nothing from any hand but his.
Aug. 17. This is, I think, almost the last entry I shall make. Another
fortnight and I shall be too weak to hold the pen—if, indeed, I am still
here.
Sept. 5. Another attack. Strange how this weary body bears up
against all this pain. Would that it were over; and yet, my poor,
poor boy. . . . He too, is almost worn out; night and day he never
leaves me. . . . I take the things from his hand, but I cannot taste
them now—nothing but lead. . . .
Sept. 27*. Farewell my husband—my darling—my own precious
Willie. Think of me—come soon to me. God bless you—God
comfort you—my darling—my own.

In the hand of Mr. Anderton.
   This day my darling died.
   Oct. 12th, 1856.   W.A.

SECTION IV

1—*Memorandum of Mr. Henderson.*

In the following certificate you will perceive that the lady is described
as of " Acacia Cottage, Kensington." The identity of the name with
that given by both Julie and Leopoldo, as the proper designation of
the Baron's " medium," confirmed my suspicion that it was in fact to
the girl Rosalie that the Baron was married under that name, notwithstanding the strong opinion of Julie as to the impossibility of such
being the case. Still, however, it was possible that this might, after
all, be a mere coincidence; and I therefore proceeded to make such
enquiries as seemed most likely to elucidate the point. I had considerable difficulty in finding the house, which two or three years back
was included in the regular numbering of the row of similar tenements
in which it stands; but I at last succeeded in identifying it. I found
the landlady a very deaf old person, whose memory was evidently

---

* Written in pencil, the characters barely legible from weakness.

1854. Marriage solemnised at the Parish Church in the Parish of Kensington, in the County of Middlesex.

No.	Date	Name and Surname	Age	Condition	Residence	Father's Name	Rank or Profession of Father
61	6 Nov. 1854.	Carl Schwartz.	Full Age.	Bachelor.	Windermere Villas, Notting Hill.	Carl Schwartz.	Gentleman.
		Charlotte Brown.	Full Age.	Spinster.	Acacia Cottage.	Not known	Not known.

Married in the Parish Church according to the rites and ceremonies of the Established Church, *after banns*, by me,
J. W. Edwards, B.A.

This marriage was solemnised between us :   In the presence of us :
    Carl Schwartz ⎫   Thomas Jones ⎫
    Charlotte Brown ⎭   Frederick Coleman ⎭

The above is a copy from the Register of Marriages belonging to this Church.
Witness my hand, 7th November, 1854.
R. Johnson.

failing, and was at first unable to extract from her any kind of information on the subject, except that " she had had a great many lodgers, and couldn't be expected to know about all of them." In the course of a second visit, however, I succeeded in persuading her to favour me with a sight of her books, and looking back to October and November, 1854, I found the sum of £2 5s. entered as payment from Miss C. Brown of three weeks' rent, from the 18th October to the 8th November.* On further examining the books, I found that at this time, while the other lodger was charged sundry sums for fire, Miss Brown, though occupying the principal sitting-room, had no fire at all during the whole time of her tenancy, though the commencement of November in that year was unusually cold. There were also sundry other little charges invariable in the other cases, but omitted in the case of Miss Brown ; and at length, on these things being pointed out to her, the old lady managed to remember that the rooms had been taken by a gentleman for a lady who was to give lessons in drawing. The gentleman had paid the three weeks' rent in advance, and had specially requested that they might be kept vacant for her, as the time of her arrival was uncertain. He had also begged that any letters or messages for her should be sent to a certain address immediately. After a great deal of searching, this address was at length found, and proved to be the square glazed card which I enclose.

2—Letters or messages for Miss Brown to be forwarded immediately to care of

Baron R**.
Post Office, Notting Hill.

* Compare Sections II, 2 and 5 ; and III, 1.

The old lady further stated that she never saw the gentleman again, and that she had never seen the lady at all. In fact, after payment of the money, nothing further had been heard of either of the parties concerned ; and as no inquiries had been made for Miss Brown, the subject had altogether passed from her mind.

Being thus pretty well satisfied as to the identity of Madame R**, my next care was to trace the proceedings of the Baron between the time of his marriage and the death of his wife, which took place, as you are aware, in London, about two and a half years subsequently ; the insurances having been effected, as you well know, at about the middle of this period. The information afforded me by Dr. Jones, the medical man who signed the certificate to your office in connection with the policy on the life of Madame R**, first gave me the required clue, and you will, I think, find in the depositions immediately following, sufficient, at all events, to justify, if not to corroborate, the suspicions which first gave rise to my enquiries. It is certainly unfortunate that here, too—as in the case of Mr. Aldridge, whose letter first roused these suspicions—the witness on whose evidence the principal stress must be laid, is not one whose testimony would probably carry much weight with a jury. Such, however, as it is, I have felt it my duty to lay it before you ; and I will now leave it, with such other as I have been able to collect, to tell its own tale.

3—*Statement of Mrs. Whitworth.*

My name is Jane Whitworth. I am a widow, and gain my living by letting apartments at Bognor, Sussex. The principal season at Bognor is during the Goodwood races, and there are very few visitors there in the autumn and winter. On the 6th October, 1854, I let the whole upper part of my house to a lady and gentleman, who arrived there late that evening. They gave some foreign name; I forget what. It was some long German name. They did not give the name at first. Not till I asked for it. I don't know that the gentleman was particularly unwilling. I said I wanted it for my bill ; and he laughed, and said it did not matter—anything would do. Then I said, if letters came, and he said :—" Oh ! There won't be any letters," and he went on reading the paper. I went down stairs, and as I was going down he rang, and I went back, and he told me of his own accord. That was at the end of the first week, when I was making out my bill. They said they intended remaining for some weeks. It was the gentleman who said this. The lady took no part in the business, and seemed out of spirits, and very much afraid of her husband. He settled with me to take the apartments at thirty shillings a week. He was to remain as long as he liked. Not beyond the next race week, of course. We never let over the race week. He also made an agreement with me about board. I was to find for him and the lady, and the servant, for £2 15s. a week. That was without wine, beer or spirits. It is not a usual

arrangement. We do it sometimes—not often. The gentleman said
it was because his wife was not well, and could not be troubled. The
servant was his. It was a maid. She did not come with them. The
gentleman hired her at Brighton. That is not a usual arrangement.
Certainly not. I never made such a one before, and I told him so.
He said it was because he was so particular about his servants. He
said he never would live where the servants were not under his own
hand—where he could not turn them away. I said I did not like it,
it was not the custom. He said he was sorry, but he could not take
the apartments without it, and then I gave way. Afterwards he followed me down stairs, and gave me to understand it was something
about his wife. At first, I thought she was not quite right in her head.
That was from what he told me. I said I should be afraid to have her
in the house, but he laughed, and said it was not that. I then supposed
it must be temper. He was very pleasant about it. He was always
very pleasant to me. I don't know what he may have been to other
people. I always had my money to the day, and he was always pleasant.
I can't say better than that. He got a servant a few days after they
came. I did not turn away my own. I had none at the time. The
season being over, it was a great chance whether I let again, and I sent
my servant away and did for myself. A charwoman did for the
gentleman till he got a servant. He got one from Brighton. I
recommended two or three in Bognor, but they did not suit. The one
he got was a girl about twenty. Her name was Sarah Something. I
did not think much of her. I used sometimes to think my tea and
sugar went very fast. I never caught her taking anything. She was
very quiet and civil-spoken. She stayed with the gentleman about a
month ; not quite. She was sent away for giving the lady a dose of
physic in her arrowroot to make her sick. The lady was very bad
indeed. We thought she would have died. She was dreadfully sick,
and had the cholera awfully bad. This was the 9th of December.*
I know it from my books. The gentleman sent out for brandy and
several things, and they are down in my book. On the following
morning he sent for some stuff from the chemist.† Before that he had
given her some medicine himself. I don't know what it was. He had
a lot of chemicals and things. He kept them in a back room. The
lady had a doctor. Not at first. Not till the Monday after she was
ill. I asked him to send for one, but he said he was a doctor himself.
She continued very ill, and on the Sunday night I asked him again.
He said if she was not better the next morning he would. I wanted him
to send for Dr. Pesketh or Dr. Thompson, but he would not. He
said they were no good. I have always heard them very highly spoken
of. Dr. Pesketh I have always heard of as a first-rate doctor. He is
since dead. Dr. Thompson is a very good doctor too ; but Dr.
Pesketh, perhaps, had the most practice. I don't think the gentleman

* Compare Mrs. Anderton's Journal, Dec. 9, p. 501.

† On enquiry I find this to have been the decoction of Peruvian bark.—R.H.

THE NOTTING HILL MYSTERY

knew anything about either of them. He sent for a Dr. Jones, who was in lodgings in the Steyne. I believe he lived in London. He prescribed for the lady while he stayed in Bognor. He went away the week after. The gentleman heard of him through a friend of mine in the Steyne. He asked me to find out whether there was no London doctor in the place. He would not have anyone who belonged to the place. He said country doctors were no good. The lady got better, but very slowly. She was ill several weeks. When she was strong enough they went away. He was very attentive to her. Never left her alone for a minute hardly. She did not seem very fond of him. I think she was afraid of him, but I don't know why. He was very kind to her, and always particularly civil. Sometimes she seemed quite put out like by his civility. I thought sometimes she would have flown out at him. She never did fly out. He always seemed able to stop her. I don't know how he did it. He never said anything ; only looked at her ; but it was quite enough. I thought she must have been doing something wrong, and he had brought her to Bognor to be out of the way. I do not know exactly what made me think so. It was the way they went on, and what he said to me. He never told me so. It was from the things he said. I did not talk much to the lady. I thought her very ungrateful when he was so kind. Then she was hardly ever alone. Only once when the gentleman went out for something. Then she was left about an hour. She was writing part of the time. She borrowed writing materials of me. There were none in the sitting-room. There usually were, but the gentleman sent the inkstand downstairs. He said it was sure to be upset. I lent the lady the things, and she gave me two letters for the post. She did not say anything to me ; only asked me to post them immediately. One was addressed to Notting Hill. I noticed that because I have a sister living there ; the other was to some theatre. I forget where. It struck me, because I thought it odd that a lady should write to a theatre. I didn't think it was right. I would rather not say what I thought. Well, it was that she was connected with someone there. Improperly, of course. The letter was not addressed to a man. It was " Miss Somebody," but that might be a blind. I thought this might account for her behaviour to her husband. I was very angry. A woman has no right to go on so. It is particularly bad when she has such a good husband. I did not say this to her. I did not notice the address till I got down-stairs. I kept the letters, and told the gentleman when he came in. He seemed very much vexed. He took the letters, and was very much obliged to me. He put the letter to the theatre into the fire without opening it. The other he said he would post himself. I don't know whether he did post it, or not. I suppose so, of course. I think he spoke to the lady about it. I am sure he did, for that night when I went up, I could see she had been crying, and she would never speak to me again. She spoke English quite well. The letters were addressed in English. When she spoke to the gentleman, it was usually in some foreign language, but she could speak English perfectly. I do not know what became of the girl, Sarah. I think she went into service again, in Brighton. I know the gentleman gave her a character. He was very kind to her. He was always very kind. He was the pleasantest and most civil-spoken gentleman I ever met, and I think his wife behaved very bad to him.

4—*Statement of Dr. Jones, of Gower Street, Bedford Square.**

I am a physician, residing in Gower Street, Bedford Square. In the beginning of December, 1854, I was suffering from a severe cold, and being unable to shake it off, went for a fortnight to the sea for change of air. I selected Bognor, because I had been in the habit of spending my holidays there for two or three years. I was lodging in the Steyne. Some few days after my arrival, I received a message requesting me to call and see a lady who was dangerously ill at a lodging in another part of the town. At first I declined to go, not wishing to interfere with the established practitioners of the place. A gentleman then called upon me, who gave the name of the Baron R**. He informed me that the lady in question was his wife, and that she was dangerously ill from the effects of a considerable quantity of emetic tartar, administered to her by the maid. He was very urgent with me to attend, saying that he was in the greatest anxiety about his wife, and that he could not in such a case sufficiently rely upon the skill of any country doctor. He pressed me so strongly that I at length consented to accompany him to his lodgings. I found the patient in a very exhausted condition, and evidently suffering from the effects of some irritant poison. From what the Baron told me, the symptoms were much abated, but the purging still continued, accompanied with severe griping pains and profuse perspirations. I learned from the Baron that, being himself a good amateur chemist, and having accidentally discovered at the outset the origin of his wife's illness, he had so far treated her himself, rather than trust to the chance of a country physician. He described his treatment, which appeared to me perfectly correct. On becoming satisfied of the cause of the disturbance, he first promoted vomiting as much as possible by the exhibition of tepid water, and afterwards of warm water, with a small quantity of mustard. When no more food appeared to be left in the stomach, he then administered large quantities of a saturated infusion of green tea, of which he had a few pounds at hand for his own drinking, finally, at the time of my arrival was exhibiting considerable doses of decoction of Peruvian bark ; both which remedies are recommended by Professor Taylor in cases of antimonial poisoning. Their action left no doubt on my mind as to the origin of the symptoms ; but by desire of the Baron I proceeded to analyse with him portions of the vomited and excreted matter, as also a portion of the arrowroot in

* Compare Section III, 2.

which the tartarised antimony was supposed to have been administered. To all of these we together applied the usual tests,—viz. : nitric acid, ferrocyanide of potassium, and hydrosulphuret of ammonia,—and succeeded in ascertaining beyond doubt the presence of antimony in all three. The quantity, however, appears to have been small. So far as we could ascertain, there could not have been more than one, or at the most two grains of tartarised antimony in the arrowroot, of which not much more than three parts had been eaten. I cannot account for the violent action of so small a quantity. I have frequently administered much larger doses in cases of inflammation of the lungs without ill effect. Two grains is by no means an unusual dose when intended to act as an emetic ; but the action of antimony varies greatly with different constitutions. Having certified ourselves of the presence of the suspected poison, the question was, as to the person by whom it had been administered. The Baron said that he had no doubt it was a trick on the part of the servant maid, between whom and her mistress there had been some dispute a few days since. We therefore determined on taxing her with it ; but before doing so, proceeded to examine a bottle of prepared tartar emetic, which, as the Baron informed me, he kept for his own use, being subject to digestive derangement. He was, I believe, addicted to the pleasures of the table, and was in the habit of taking an occasional emetic. The bottle was not in its usual place, but was standing on the table at the side of the dressing-case in which it was usually kept. It was labelled, " The emetic. One teaspoonful to be taken as directed." I remarked that it should be labelled " poison," and the Baron quite agreed with me, and immediately wrote the word in large characters on a piece of paper and gummed it round the bottle. We then weighed the contents of the bottle, from which three doses only had been taken by the Baron, and, on comparing the results, we found that a quantity equivalent to about one grain and a half of the tartarised antimony had been abstracted in excess of this amount. The servant maid was the only person besides the Baron who usually had access to the apartment ; and we at once sent for her and taxed her with having administered it to Madame R** in the arrowroot before mentioned. My own counsel was to give her immediately in charge, but the Baron pointed out, very justly, that there was nothing to show the girl that she was doing anything that could possibly affect life ; and that, in the absence of any motive for such a crime, it was only fair to conclude that nothing was intended beyond a foolish practical joke. He said the same to the girl, and spoke to her very kindly indeed. At first she altogether denied it, and pretended to be quite astonished at such an imputation. The Baron, however, looked steadily at her, and said, " Take care, Sarah ! Remember what I said to you only three days ago." She did not attempt then to deny it any longer, but said she was very sorry, but she hoped the Baron would forgive her. The Baron said he could not possibly retain her in his service, and she then begged of him not to send her away without a character. At this time I interfered, and said he would be very wrong to send her into any other family after playing such a trick. She again protested she had meant no harm, and the subject then dropped, the Baron saying he would take time to consider of it. From that time I attended Madame R★★ until my return to London, when she was clearly recovering. I did not enter into any conversation with her, as she seemed very reserved and of an unsociable disposition. The Baron seemed an unusually attentive husband. Talking over the subject of the seizure a day or two afterwards, he informed me that the death of his wife would also have been a severe loss in a pecuniary point of view, as if she lived she would inherit a considerable fortune. I asked him why he did not insure her life, and he said he should now certainly do so, but had not before thought of it. He called upon me about two months later, in passing through town, and informed me that he intended to travel abroad for some months. I recommended the German baths, and on his objecting to the crowds of English there, suggested Greisbach or Rippoldsau, in the Black Forest, where Englishmen are rarely to be encountered. It was too early for either place at that time, and I recommended the South of France until the season was sufficiently advanced. I did not see him again till October, 1855, when he again called upon me with Madame R★★, who seemed perfectly restored, and of whom I had no difficulty in reporting most favourable to the ──── Life Assurance Association, as also some weeks late to the ──── Life Office of Dublin, when applied to for my professional opinion. I think Madame R★★'s was an excellent life, and there could be no better proof of it than her entire recovery, in the course of a very few months, or indeed weeks, from so severe an illness. The sensitiveness to antimony would not affect this opinion. Indeed, Professor Taylor, in his work on poisons, points out distinctly the " idiosyncratic " action of antimony and other medicinals on certain constitutions, as " conferring on an ordinary medicinal dose a poisonous instead of a curative action." I have a copy of his work now before me, in which he says that " daily experience teaches us that some persons are more powerfully affected than others by an ordinary dose of opium, arsenic, *antimony* and other substances"; and again, in considering the probable amount of the " fatal dose," he speaks of " that ever-varying condition of idiosyncracy, in which, as it is well known, there is a state of constitution more liable to be affected by antimonial compounds than other individuals apparently in the same conditions as to health, age, etc." I did not, therefore, nor do I now, consider the sensitiveness of Madame R★★'s constitution to that medicine any objection to her life, especially in view of the immense vitality shown by her recovery. With regard to the sleep-walking, I have had no hint from the Baron of such a propensity on the part of Madame R★★. Certainly it was never suggested that she could have poisoned herself in that way. Indeed the servant girl admitted the act. The mode of Madame R★★'s death does not in any degree shake my confidence in my former opinion, as such an occurrence might have happened, though by no means likely to do so, to any one in the habit of walking in their sleep, a propensity which in Madame R**'s case I had no means of ascertaining. I have been enabled to be thus precise in my statement, from the fact that the interesting nature of the case led me to make a special memorandum of it in my diary, from which the above is taken. I shall therefore have no difficulty in confirming any portion of it upon oath.

5—*Statement of Mrs. Throgmorton.*

Mrs. Throgmorton presents her compliments to Mr. R. Henderson, and begs to inform him that the girl Sarah Newman, who is still in her service, and continues to give entire satisfaction in every way, came to her about Christmas, 1854, with a written character from the Baron R**, then residing at Bognor, and with whom she had been as housemaid and parlourmaid for some weeks. The character given by the Baron was a most satisfactory one, but on Mrs. Throgmorton's desiring to know the reason of Sarah Newman's leaving the situation, she was informed by the Baron that it was on account of her having played a foolish trick upon her late mistress by administering an emetic to her without authority, a highly reprehensible proceeding, which rendered Mrs. Throgmorton very much indisposed to receive her into her family. On further correspondence with Sarah Newman's late master, however, Mrs. Throgmorton received the impression that the fault had, in point of fact, been chiefly on the side of Madame R**, though, of course, impossible to say so directly with respect to his own wife, and Mrs. Throgmorton therefore agreed to take Sarah Newman on trial, as she appeared truly penitent for her most reprehensible conduct, and has since proved a very valuable servant in every respect. Mrs. Throgmorton trusts that this information will be satisfactory to Mr. Henderson, as he appears interested in Sarah Newman's welfare, in whom Mrs. Throgmorton herself takes great interest.

Cliftonville.

6—*Statement of Mr. Andrews.*

" Sir,
In reply to your letter of the 25th ultimo, I beg to inform you that the girl, Sarah Newman, certainly was in my service at Brighton for a month or two in the summer of 1854, but was discharged, I think, in September of that year, for various petty thefts. She was a very interesting girl, and took us in completely, but was accidentally discovered by one of our children, and after full proof of her delinquencies, turned away without a character. My own wish was to prosecute her, which indeed I considered almost a duty to others whom she might hereafter plunder, but I was persuaded to relinquish my

intention by my wife, who had taken a great fancy to her. About two months after her dismissal, a gentleman, who gave some German name—I cannot now remember it—called to enquire our reasons for discharging her, and I then informed him of the whole case. He questioned me pretty closely as to my real opinion of the girl, stating that he was philanthropically disposed, and would give her a chance for reform, if there was any likelihood of her availing herself of it. I told him frankly my own opinion, viz : that the girl was a hardened offender; but my wife was very eager that she should have another chance, and I have very little doubt the German gentleman took her. He was, so far as I remember, a stout, good-natured looking man, and he had with him a young lady whom he left in the carriage, and who was, he said, his wife. I think the name you mention, Baron **, is the same name as that given—or at least something like it—but cannot be quite sure. I am,

Dear Sir,
Faithfully yours,
CHARLES ANDREWS."

P.S.—My wife begs me to ask that should you know anything of the after-career of her protégée, you will kindly communicate it to us.

R. Henderson, Esq., &c., &c., &c.,
Clement's Inn, W.C.

7—Statement of Sarah Newman.

N.B.—This statement was not obtained without considerable difficulty, and must be taken for whatever it is worth. The girl was naturally anxious to be secured against the possible consequence of her own admissions, and I only at last succeeded in inducing her to speak out by means both of a promise on the part of Mrs. Throgmorton not to discharge her, and a threat of police interference, if she did not confess the whole truth. I have, myself, no doubt whatever of the correctness of her statement as it now stands, and it is, as you will see, corroborated in several very important particulars, but whether it could be produced before a jury, or, if it were so, what effect it would have upon their minds, are both very doubtful questions.

R.H.

My name is Sarah Newman. I was in the service of Mr. Andrews at Brighton for three months. I was discharged by him for stealing tea and sugar. Mr. Andrews wanted to take the law of me, but my mistress would not let him. My Mistress would have kept me on, but master said No. She was always very kind to me, and it was very ungrateful of me to rob her. I would never do so again. ℂMy present mistress is very kind to me, too. I have never robbed her of a pin. I declare to goodness I have not, nor I never will steal from anybody again. I have often wanted to tell Mrs. Andrews so since, but I did not know

where she was. I did not say it to her when I left. I felt quite hard
like, because of master. I was out of a place for two months after
that. No one would take me without a character. At last a friend
at Bognor told me of a gentleman, and I got her to speak to him.
It was the Baron. He came to see me one day when he was at
Brighton. He insisted on knowing all about me—where I had been
and why I had left Mr. Andrews. He was very kind, and said it
was hard a poor girl should be ruined for one false step. He said
if I would promise never to steal again he would give me a trial.
I promised him faithfully, and he at last took me down to Bognor
with him. I do not know whether he made any inquiries about
me. I think not. He did not tell me he had. I meant to keep
my promise. Indeed I did, and I did keep it, almost. I mean I
only took one little thing, and I really did not think that was stealing.
Nothing was ever locked up. The Baron always insisted on having the
tea-chest and other things left open in case he wanted some. I never
took any. I might have taken a great deal, but I did not. I used to
think sometimes things were left on purpose to tempt me, but of course
that was fancy. Often there were coppers left about, but I never
touched them. I did take one thing at last. I did not think it was
stealing. It was only some orange-marmalade. I am very fond of
sweet things. One day there was a pot of orange-marmalade. It was
left on the table. It was after they had gone away from breakfast. It
looked so nice. I just put in my finger. That was all. I declare to
goodness that was all. I did not even taste it. The Baron came back
and caught me. He did not say anything. He just shut the door
close and walked straight up to me. I was so frightened I could not
move. He took hold of my wrist and held up my hand. I burst out
crying. He said it was no use crying; I had deceived him and must
go. He said if he did his duty he ought to give me up to the police.
I said indeed I had taken nothing, but only that little taste of sweets.
He said who would believe me with my character? He spoke very
kind but very stern, and I was dreadfully frightened. I begged of
him not to give me up, and he said he would give me one chance
more; but I must go away. I said if he turned me out without a
character I might as well drown myself at once. I begged him to let
me stay; but he said that was impossible. Then I begged him not
to say why I was sent away. He said what else could he say? I
begged him again very hard. At last he said he would think over it.
He said he would try and make some other excuse for my going, but I
must go next day, positive. He told me if he did make an excuse for
me to be very careful not to contradict him. I was very grateful to
him. He is a kind good gentleman, and I shall always bless him for
it. I did not go next day. I was kept by my mistress's illness. She
was very bad indeed. I did all I could for her. I hoped the Baron
had forgotten and would let me stay. He sent for me two or three days
afterward. There was another gentleman with him. It was the

doctor. He charged me with having given some stuff to my mistress to make her sick. Of course I denied it. I never gave her anything. I never had any quarrel with her at all. She was always very good-natured to me, but I did not like her much. I don't know why. I think it was because she did not like master. I said I had given her nothing. No more I had. I never saw the bottle, and don't know what it was. I cannot read at all. I saw master look at me, and he said something about two or three days ago. I knew then that he was making an excuse to send me away. He made signs at me to abide by what he said, and I did abide by it. The other gentleman was very hard, but of course he did not know. What the Baron said was given as a reason for my going away. That was all. The real reason was my taking the marmalade. If you ask the Baron he will tell you so. I hope you will tell him how grateful I am for his kindness to me.

SECTION V

1—*Memorandum by Mr. Henderson.*

We have now reached a point in this mysterious story at which I must again direct your attention most particularly to the coincidences of dates, etc., on which, indeed, depends entirely, as I have before said, the only solution at which I have found it possible to arrive.

The length to which these depositions have run has obliged me to divide them into distinct sections, each of which should bear more directly upon some particular phase of the case. For this purpose I have taken, as you will have perceived, first the early history of Mrs. Anderton, and as we may, I think, fairly assume, of Madame R★★ also, thus establishing, at the outset, the initiatory link of that chain of connection between these two extraordinary cases, which, inexplicable as either is in itself, will nevertheless, I cannot but imagine, each help to elucidate the other. The second division placed us in possession of the histories both of Mrs. Anderton and Madame R★★ up to the point at which the thread of their singular destinies crossed; showing, also, how the Baron became aware of his wife's probable relationship to Mrs. Anderton, and of the benefit thereby accruing to her upon the death, without issue, of her sister and Mr. Anderton. The third section deals with the first illness of Madame R★★, to the date and circumstances of which I felt it right to direct your most particular attention.

In the fourth division of the evidence we then reviewed the circumstances attending the fatal illness of Mrs. Anderton, which led to her husband's arrest on suspicion of murder, and finally to his suicide, while awaiting investigation. A considerable portion of the evidence connected with this phase of the subject I have thought it best to keep back for insertion in that division of the case which bears more particularly upon the conduct and death of Mr. Anderton, and which will follow that on which we are about to enter. The narrative, therefore, of Mrs. Anderton's last illness has been thus far confined to the mention of it in the unfortunate lady's own diary, with the note at its termination, in which her husband records the fact of her decease. With this, however, I have coupled an account, drawn partly from an earlier portion of the same diary, and partly from the statement of the medical man by whom she was at the time attended, of a previous illness very similar in general character to that by which she was finally carried off, and apparently of an equally unaccountable description. The object with which I have thus placed in juxtaposition the first attacks respectively of Madame R** and Mrs. Anderton will probably be sufficiently apparent. I have now to direct your attention to a second illness of Madame R**, occurring, under what I cannot but feel to be most suspicious circumstances, but a very few months before her demise.

In proceeding with this portion of the case, the extreme importance attaching to a thorough and correct appreciation of the dates of the various occurrences will become more obvious at every step, and to them I must again request your utmost attention. I had at first proposed to submit to you in tabular form the singular coincidences to which I allude, but on reflection, such a course appeared objectionable, as tending to place too strongly before you a view of the subject with which I must confess myself thoroughly dissatisfied. I have, therefore, preferred leaving entirely to yourselves the comparison of the various dates, etc., limiting myself strictly to a verification of their accuracy. In many instances this has been no easy task, and more particularly in establishing satisfactorily the exact date (5th April, 1856), at which the symptoms of Madame R**'s second illness first appeared, wherein I have experienced a difficulty only compensated by the importance of the result.

I have, therefore, to request that the depositions here following may be carefully compared with the concluding portion of Mrs. Anderton's diary, and also with the statement of Dr. Dodsworth. In making this comparison you will notice, besides the points I have already referred to respecting dates, various discrepancies between facts as actually occurring and as represented to Mr. and Mrs. Anderton by the Baron. These I need not here particularise, as they will be sufficiently obvious on a perusal of the depositions themelves, but it is as well to draw your attention generally to them, as they seem to have a significant bearing upon other parts of the case.

I must request you also to bear in mind the relation in which the Baron and his wife were supposed to stand towards each other previously to their marriage, and will now proceed to lay before you the depositions relating, as I have said, to the second illness of the latter.

2—Statement of Mrs. Brown.

My name is Jane Brown. I am a widow, and my poor dear husband was a clerk in the city. I don't know whose house. I did know but I forget. My memory is very bad. I live in Russell Place. The house is my own, not hired. My poor dear husband left it to me in his will. I sometimes let it off in lodgings. Not always. Only when I can get quiet lodgers. Last year* I let the first and second floors to Baron R**. The ground floor was let to Dr. Marsden. He has had it several years. He does not live there. He has a practice near London. He comes to Russel Place every Monday and Friday to see his patients. He used to live with us. That was in my poor dear husband's lifetime. Baron R** took the rest of the house except the attics. I lived there myself. I cannot remember when the Baron came. It was some time in February or March. I am sure I cannot remember. I have no means of ascertaining. I don't keep any accounts. My poor dear husband always kept the accounts. I have kept none since he died. I dare say I lose money by it, but I can't help it. I have no head for it. I am pretty sure it was in February or March. I think about the beginning of March.† There was no other lodger then. Not till my son went away from home again. He was away from home then. He came home some time in March or April. I suppose it was in March. He came from Melbourne to Liverpool. He was at home for some weeks. I can't tell how many. He went away again in April, or it might have been May. I am almost sure it was not later than May. Not so late, I think. Mrs. Troubridge could tell you. Richard married her daughter. Richard is my son. He married Ellen Troubridge. That was while he was at home last year. They had been engaged ever so long. He came home on purpose to marry her. He had got a promise of something at Melbourne, and was obliged to go back directly. He worked his passage home from Melbourne. I do not know what ship he came in. I don't think he shipped in his own name. I forget why it was. Something about not liking to have it known. I don't know why not; I don't know at all what name he took. I cannot remember when he came home or when he went. I do not know when he left Melbourne. He brought home one paper. There is only a small piece of it left. He was with me all the time he was at home except Saturdays and Sundays. He used to go down to Brighton then to see Ellen. She was in a shop there. He used to go by the excursion train and stay with her mother from Saturday to Monday. All the rest of the time he was with me. That is all I can tell you about him. The other lodger was a friend of his. He had known him in Australia. He asked him to his wedding. That was at our house. It was on a Monday, and he came the Saturday before. They all came up together from Brighton. The Baron let us

---

* 1856.—R.H.

† Clearly so. The Baron was in Dublin on 25th Feb.—R.H.

use his rooms. He went away somewhere to give his lady change of air. I think it was because she had been ill. I cannot be sure. She was ill several times at my house. She died there. I forget when was the first time she was ill there. It was while my son was in England. I remember talking to him about it. He was away from home at the time. There was no one in the house but myself. I remember it because I was so frightened. There was nobody at all. Not even a servant. I generally have a servant. I was without one then for two or three months. I got a charwoman to come in the day. The reason was my servant got tipsy. She had to be taken away by the police and I was afraid for a long while to get another. I can't at all remember when that was. I think it must have been before the Baron came. I can't be sure. I am quite sure it was before Madame R** was taken ill. I am sure of that because I remember well how frightened I was. I think Dr. Marsden attended Madame R**. He used to be very friendly with the Baron. Everybody liked him. He was so good-natured and so very kind to his wife. We did not think so much of her. She was very quiet, but she did not seem to care much about him. She seemed frightened like. I sometimes thought she was not quite right in her head. The Baron was always kind to her. He was good-natured with everybody. I never heard him say a hard word of anyone but once. That was of young Aldridge. He was Richard's friend who lodged with us.* He made a noise and disturbed Madame R**. He came home one night quite intoxicated, and the Baron asked me to give him notice. He said if Mr. Aldridge did not go he must. Of course I gave him notice directly. He said it was all spite. Of course I knew that was not true. He said he was not drunk, but the policeman found him lying on the door-step. I forget what he said. It was some foolish story about the Baron. I do not know of any reason why they should have quarrelled. I remember he said something once about Madame R** walking in her sleep. I don't know what it was. I don't think it could have had anything to do with it. Of course it could not. The Baron complained of being disturbed. That was all. I do not remember that I was ever disturbed myself. His room was next to mine. I might have been disturbed without remembering it . I certainly was that night he came home intoxicated. He might have disturbed Madame R** and I slept through it. I sleep heavy sometimes. I forget when this was and when he left the house. I cannot remember the exact dates of anything. My poor dear husband always did everything of that sort for me. He was a very exact man. I have no books or papers of any kind to which I could refer. This is all I can tell you.

---

* This portion of Mrs. Brown's evidence affects more particularly the part of the case to be hereafter referred to in Part vii; but I have thought it best to preserve it intact.—R.H.

3—*Statement of Mrs. Troubridge.*

My name is Ellen Troubridge. My husband is a seafaring man. He is captain of a small collier. We live at Shoreham, near Brighton. I have one daughter, whose name is Ellen. She is married to a man of the name of Richard Brown. He is in Australia. He went out to Australia in 1856. I forget the exact date. It was some time in April or May. The ship's name was the Maria Somes. She sailed from Gravesend. My daughter was married on the 14th of April. That was not very long before they sailed. She had been engaged to young Brown for three or four years. He came home on purpose to marry her. I don't remember exactly when he came home. It must have been about a month before. Something of that kind. He was in a great hurry to get out again. He wanted to marry by licence, so as to be quicker, but I told him it was a foolish expense. He had the banns put up the first Sunday he was at home. I think it was the first, but cannot be quite sure. My daughter was then in service. She was at a shop in Brighton. During the week she used to sleep at a friend's house, and on Saturdays she used to come home to us for Sundays. Brown always used to come down on Saturdays. He used to come by the cheap excursion train. He used to go to Brighton and call for Nelly, and walk with her to Shoreham. He used to walk back with her early Monday morning, and go on to town. He never came at other times. It was no good. Nelly was only at home Sundays. He wanted her to leave and go to his mother's. She would not leave the shop till her time was out. I would not let him be at Brighton. I was afraid people might talk. So far as I know, he was at home all the rest of the time. The marriage took place from Mrs. Brown's house. She had a lodger then—a foreigner, I think. He went out of town for two or three days, and lent her his rooms. After the wedding young Brown and my daughter went to Southend for a few days. I cannot exactly say how long. About a week or a fortnight. On the Saturday before they sailed we all went down to Gravesend to meet them and see them off. The ship was to have sailed on the Sunday. We all went to Rosherville, and slept at Gravesend that night. I had some friends there who gave us beds. Mrs. Brown went back on Sunday, but I stayed. A young man by the name of Aldridge was with us. He was a friend of Brown's. I did not much like him. He went back with Mrs. Brown. I think he took lodgings in her house. I cannot call to mind the exact day young Brown came home, I think it must have been some time in March.

4—*Statement of Dr. Marsden.*

My name is Anthony Marsden. I am a physician, and formerly resided at Mrs. Brown's house, in Russell Place. Some three or four years ago I found the atmosphere of London beginning to tell upon my health, and determined to remove into the suburbs. I bought a small practice in the neighbourhood of St. John's Wood, and gave up the greater portion of my London patients. I was, however, desirous of not altogether relinquishing that connection, and with this object rented two rooms at Mrs. Brown's, where I might be consulted by such patients as I still retained in that neighbourhood. I used to drive up for this purpose every Monday and Thursday morning. I had been doing this for some time, when the first and second floor apartments were taken by the Baron R**. I did not at first much like him. I thought him an impostor. He seemed, however, to wish to make my acquaintance, and I found that he was, at all events, a very highly informed man on all matters of science. We had frequent conversations respecting mesmerism. He certainly seemed himself to be a believer in it. Were I not myself thoroughly satisfied of its impossibility, I am not at all sure but that he might have convinced me on the subject. I am quite unable to account for many of the phenomena exhibited. They were, however, of course, to be accounted for in some way. He seemed a very excellent chemist, and we used at times to pursue our investigations together. There was a small room at the back of the house, on the basement floor, which he used as a laboratory. He invited me to make use of it, and I was frequently there. He was always engaged in experiments of one kind or another, and had various ingenious projects in hand. In the laboratory was a large assortment of chemicals and medicines of various kinds. In the case of poor patients, I have sometimes asked him to make up a prescription, and he has done so. At the time at which I knew him, he was engaged in a series of experiments on the metals, and more especially on mercury, antimony, lead and zinc. I think he must have had almost every preparation of these that is made. I believe that his researches were for the purpose of finding a specific against the disease so prevalent among painters, which is known by the name of " lead colic." The laboratory was at the back of the house, and quite detached from all the other rooms. There was an open space between it and the rest of the house, with only a passage communicating with the offices. This passage was shut off by a glass door, and there was a wooden door at the end into the laboratory. Both these doors were always kept closed. They were not usually locked. I told the Baron I thought they should be, but he said no one would go there. He had a weight put on the laboratory door to close it. The glass door had a spring already. I frequently made use of his laboratory : sometimes when he was absent. I might go there with or without him, whenever I pleased. There was no attempt at concealing from me anything whatever that was done there. It was all quite open. I attended Madame R** through greater part of her illness. It was a very long affair, and of a singular character. I cannot be at all certain as to the date at which it commenced. I was not regularly called in at the time, and did not notice it in my book. The Baron only consulted me in a friendly way about it, two or three days afterwards. It was certainly as much as that. I think it was the third day. I cannot be sure of that, but I am quite sure it was at least the second. By being the second day, I mean that at least one clear day had intervened between the night on which she was ill and the day on which I was consulted by the Baron. I cannot swear to more than one, but I think it must have been. From what the Baron told me of the symptoms, I remember concluding it to be a case of English cholera, but she was almost recovered at the time I first heard of it, and I did not prescribe for her. About a fortnight or three weeks after this she had another slight attack, for which the Baron himself also prescribed. He acquainted me on my visit to town with the course he had pursued, and I entirely concurred in his treatment of the case. The attack, however, returned, I think more than once, and he then asked me to see and prescribe for her. I first saw her professionally on the 23rd of May, 1856.* This was two days after the third or fourth attack, which occurred on the night of the 21st of May. As soon as I regularly took up her case, I made notes of it in my diary. Extracts from this are enclosed (*vide 5 herewith*) showing the progress of the case from time to time. I attended her throughout her illness. The attacks occurred, as will be seen from my diary, about every fortnight. They increased in intensity up to the 10th of October, 1856. At this time she was apparently, for three or four days, almost *in articulo mortis*, and I was unable to hold out any hope of her recovery. Another attack would certainly have been fatal. Happily the disease appeared to have spent itself, and at the expiration no renewal of the more acute symptoms was experienced. From this date Madame R** progressed steadily but slowly to convalescence, and would no doubt ultimately have entirely recovered, but for the unfortunate accident which put an end to her life. Madame R**'s case was one of great difficulty. It was apparently one of chronic gastritis; but its recurrence in an acute form at stated intervals was a very abnormal incident. The case presented, in fact, all the more prominent features of that of chronic antimonial poisoning recorded by Dr. Mayerhofer in Heller's Archiv :, 1846, and alluded to by Professor Taylor in his work on Poisons, p. 539. There were also strong points of general resemblance to the other cases of M'Mullen and Hardman, quoted by Professor Taylor at the same page, and recorded in Guy's Hospital Reports for October, 1857. As matters progressed, I took the opportunity of pointing this out as delicately as I could to the Baron, and asked if he had any suspicions of foul play. He seemed at first almost amused by the suggestion; but upon further consideration was inclined to take a graver view of the matter. We went carefully through the cases in question, the Baron translating that of Dr. Mayerhofer for my benefit, as I was not a German scholar. At his suggestion, we determined to analyse the various excretions, etc., and an examination was accordingly instituted in the Baron's laboratory. He was always very particular in keeping up the supply of medicine,

* Comp. journal of Mrs. Anderton, 25th May and 10th June. *Vide*, Section III, 3.

and would never allow the bottles, etc., to be thrown away. There
was therefore some remnant of every medicine that had been made up
for her. These we tested carefully, as well as the excreta, etc., both
for arsenic and antimony, but without finding the slightest trace of
either. The analysis was conducted by the Baron, who took the greatest
interest in it. I could not perhaps have done it myself. Such matters
have not come within my line of practice. In such a case I should
certainly not trust to my own manipulations. I trusted to those of the
Baron, because I knew him to be an expert practical chemist, and in
the daily habit of such operations. My own share in them was limited
to the observation of results, and their comparison with those pointed
out by Professor Taylor. I did not take any special pains to ascertain
the purity of the chemical tests employed, or of their being in fact what
they were assumed to be. That is to say, when a colourless liquid with
all the apparent characteristics of nitric acid was taken from a bottle
labelled " Nit. Ac." I took for granted that nitric acid was being
employed. Similarly, of course, with the other chemical agents. It
never occurred to me to do otherwise. Nor did I take any special
precautions to identify the matters examined. Others might certainly
have been substituted ; but if so, it must have been done by the Baron
himself. It was, perhaps, possible that he might have conducted his
investigations, under such supervision as I then exercised, with fic-
titious tests, and it was quite so to substitute other matters and mislead
me by subjecting them to a real analysis. That is to say, this would
have been possible to be done by the Baron. No one else could, under
the circumstances, have done it, or at least without his direct connivance.
I had no ground for any suspicion of the kind, nor do I see any now. I
think it most unwarrantable. Every circumstance that came under
my notice goes equally to contravene such a supposition. The Baron
was devotedly attached to his wife : he supplied her liberally with
professional advice, as also with nurses, medicine, and every necessary ;
his care for her led him to precautions which, in their incidental results,
must have inevitably exposed any attempt at the administration of
poison. During the severer period of the disorder, he had no opportunity of committing such a crime, as he universally insisted on both
food and medicine being both prepared and administered by the nurses;
he himself rendered every assistance in the endeavour to detect any
such attempt when its possibility had been suggested by myself ; and
lastly, Madame R** did not die, although the investigation had already
removed all suspicion. I think such an imputation wholly unwar-
ranted and unwarrantable from any one circumstance of the case.

5—*Extracts from Dr. Marsden's Diary.**

May 23rd. Madame R**, nausea, vomiting, tendency to diarrhœa, profuse perspiration, and general debility. Pulse low, 100. Spirits depressed. Burning pain in stomach—abdomen tender on pressure. Tongue discoloured.

26th. Madame R** slightly better—less nausea and pain.

30th. Madame R**. Improvement continued.

June 2nd. Madame R** improving.

6th. Ditto.

9th. Recurrence of symptoms on Saturday evening.† Increased nausea, vomited matter yellow with bile. Pulse low, 105. Throat sore, and slight constriction. Tongue foul.

13th. Symptoms slightly ameliorated. Treatment continued.

16th. Ditto. Tongue slightly clearer. Pulse 100.

20th. Improvement continued. Pulse slightly firmer.

23rd. Ditto.

24th. Special visit. Return of symptoms last night. Great increase of nausea and vomiting—very yellow with bile. Throat sore and tongue foul. Abdomen very tender on pressure. Slight diarrhœa. Tingling sensation in limbs.

27th. Slight improvement.

30th. Continued, but slight. Pulse firmer.

July 3rd. Improvement continued, especially in throat. Perspiration still distressing. Less tingling in limbs.

6th. Improvement continued. Pulse somewhat firmer, 110. (10th to 20th. Absent in Gloucestershire).

20th. A slight rally. Baron says attack shortly after last visit, but recovery for time more rapid.

24th. Improvement continues, but less rapid. Pulse 110.

27th. Recurrence yesterday. Vomiting, purging amounting to diarrhœa. Soreness and aphthous state of mouth and throat. Perspiration. Pain in abdomen. Complains of taste in mouth like lead. Pulse low, 115. Qy. antimony? Speak, Baron.

31st. Analysis—satisfactory. Symptoms slightly abated.

August 3rd. Improvement continued. Pulse 112, firmer.

7th. Same.

10th. Return of vomiting and purging. General aggravation of symptoms. Much prostrated.

24th, 28th, 31st. Slight improvement.

September 4th. Improvement continued, but slight.

---

* These extracts will, of course, be chiefly interesting to the medical profession, and may be passed over by the general reader. Some details are necessarily excluded. The notes, also, relating to the treatment by Dr. Marsden, not materially affecting the question at issue, which is concerned only with the symptoms of disorder, are omitted as irrelevant and therefore confusing. *Vide* note to statement of Dr. Watson, Section III, 2.

† 7th June.—R.H.

7th. Return of severe symptoms. Vomiting, extremely yellow, much bile. Diarrhœa. Pulse low and fluttering, 120. Violent perspiration. Slight wandering. Extreme soreness and constriction of throat. Slight convulsive twitchings in limbs. Great exhaustion and prostration.

10th, 14th, 18th. Very slight abatement of symptoms.

21st. Violence of symptoms increased. Pulse 125. Great prostration.

25th, 28th. Very slight amelioration. Pulse 125. Wandering.

October 1st, 4th, 8th. Symptoms slightly less severe.

11th. Aggravation of all symptoms. Pulse 132, low and fluttering. Face flushed and pale. Much convulsive twitching in limbs. Power of speech quite gone. Entire prostration. Can hardly live through night.

12th, 13th, 14th. Special visits. No perceptible change.

15th. Pulse a shade firmer, 136.

N.B.—From this date recovery slow but steady.

6—Memorandum by Mr. Henderson.

From the very vague nature of the foregoing evidence, so far as dates are concerned, it was, as you will at once perceive, no very easy task to determine the precise day of Madame R**'s first attack. To the view of the case, however, which I was even then inclined to adopt this was a matter of the last importance, and I determined to spare no effort to elucidate it if possible from the very loose data furnished by the depositions. In this I have, I think, been successful; but, as the process has been rather complicated, I must ask you to follow me through it step by step.

The difficulty of tracing the truth seemed at first sight not a little augmented by the fact that no one had been in the house but Mrs. Brown herself, whose memory, even had it afforded any clue, could not have been relied on. On further consideration, however, I began to fancy myself mistaken in this respect, and finally conceived a hope that this very fact might if properly handled, prove an assistance instead of an obstacle to my investigation. The following was the course of reasoning I pursued.

There are only two points on which Mrs. Brown appears to be certain; her son's presence in England, and her being herself alone in the house on the actual day in question. The only chances of success therefore seemed to be :—First, in ascertaining precisely the limit of time within which such a combination was possible ; and, second, in determining by a process of elimination the actual day or days on which such a combination could fall.

The result has been far more complete than at the outset of the investigation I could venture to hope.

1st. For the period of time to which our researches should be directed.

This was obviously limited by the residence of Richard Brown in England, and my first efforts were therefore directed towards determining the exact dates of his arrival and departure.

1.   On inquiry at Liverpool, I found that the only vessels which had arrived from Melbourne during the month of March, 1856, were as follows :

Ship.	Captain.	Owners.	Arrived.
James Baines.	M'Donald.	Jas. Baines & Co.	4th March
Lightning.	Enright.	„	24th „
Emma.	Underwood.	Pilkington Bros.	27th „

Of these the James Baines left Melbourne on the 28th November, and the Lightning on the 28th of December.   The exact date of sailing of the Emma I have not been able to ascertain, but it is immaterial to the case.

The fragment of newspaper preserved by Mrs. Brown has no date, nor could I at first find any clue by which it might be determined.   The last paragraph, however, commences as follows :

Seasonable Weather ! The thermometer has, for the last four days, never been lower than eighty degrees in the shade.   We wonder what our friends in England would say to singing their Ch . . . rols in such a . . . .

The remainder is torn off, but the missing syllables are clearly *Christmas Carols*, and this shows clearly that the paper must have been published after the departure of the James Baines on the 28th November. Richard Brown must therefore have come home either in the Lightning or the Emma, the earliest of which reach Liverpool on the evening of the 24th March.   The 25th of March therefore is the earliest date from which our examination need commence.

2.   From Mrs. Troubridge, mother of the young woman to whom Richard Brown was married during his stay in England, I learned that the young couple sailed for Sydney in the Maria Somes.   Mrs. Brown was unable to give me the date of this vessel's departure, but a search through the file of the Times for April, 1856, shows that she left Gravesend on the 23rd of that month.   The period to be analysed is therefore confined to the interval between the 25th March and the 25th April, 1856.

3.   During this period, as we learn from Mrs. Brown's statement, Richard Brown was at home every day except Saturdays and Sundays. These were respectively, 29th and 30th of March, and 5th, 6th, 12th, 13th, 19th and 20th of April.

4.   Dr. Marsden, in his evidence, states most distinctly that he did not see Madame R** until at least " one clear day " had elapsed after her attack.   Dr. Marsden's visits take place on the Monday and Friday of each week.   Madame R**'s seizure therefore did not occur on a Sunday.   This reduces the days on which it may have happened to the 29th March and 5th, 12th and 19th April.

5. From Mrs. Troubridge's evidence we learn that Mrs. Brown and the whole party slept at Gravesend on the Saturday night previous to the sailing of the Maria Somes. Mrs. Brown was therefore absent from town on the 19th April. The issue is thus narrowed to the 29th March and the 5th and 12th April.

6. From Mrs. Brown's statement we learn that on the Saturday and Sunday preceding the wedding her son's friend Aldridge slept at the house. The wedding took place on the 14th April. On the 12th April, therefore, Mrs. Brown was not alone. The only days, therefore, on which the occurrence, as described, could have taken place, are the 29th March and 5th April.

At this point I feared for some time that my clue was at an end. This would, however, have been most unsatisfactory, as the possible error of a week in point of date would have seriously detracted from the trustworthiness of the entire case. The only possible chance of determining the point seemed to lie in ascertaining the precise date of the servant's dismissal, and it at length occurred to me that this might be accomplished by means of the police records of the court before which she was carried. From them I found——

7. That the offence for which she was discharged was committed on Sunday, the 30th of April. On the 29th, therefore, she was still in Mrs. Brown's house. The only day, therefore, on which Madame R**'s first seizure could have taken place was stated during Richard Brown's stay in England, and on a night when Mrs. Brown was alone in the house, was the 5th of April.

The importance of this date, thus fixed, you will, I think, at once perceive

SECTION VI

I—*Memorandum by Mr. Henderson.*

WE have now arrived at a point in this extraordinary case at which I must again direct your attention to the will of the late Mr. Bolton. By this will £25,000 was, as we have seen, bequeathed to Miss Bolton (afterwards Mrs. Anderton), with a life interest, after her death, to her husband. At his decease, and failing children by his marriage with Miss Bolton, the money passed to the second sister, whom, as I have before said, we may, I think, be justified in identifying with the late Madame R**. It seems, at all events, clear, both from the circumstances attending the marriage of the Baron, and from the observation made by him at Bognor to Dr. Jones relative to the pecuniary loss he would have sustained by the death of his wife, that the Baron himself believed and was prepared to maintain this relationship, and that the various policies of assurance effected on the life of Madame R**—to the gross amount of £25,000, the exact sum in question— were intended to cover any risk of her death before that of her sister.

This is all that we need at present require.   What import should be attached to the degree of mystery with which the whole affair both of the marriage and of the assurance seems to have been so carefully surrounded will, of course, be matter for consideration when reviewing the whole circumstances of the case.   It is enough for our present purpose that the Baron clearly looked upon his wife as the sister of Mrs. Anderton, and calculated upon participation, through her, in the legacy of Mr. Bolton.   The lives of Mr. and Mrs. Anderton thus alone intervened between this legacy and the Baron's family, and we have thus established, on his part, a direct interest in their decease.

On the death of Mrs. Anderton, under the circumstances detailed in an earlier portion of the case, the life of the husband only now stood in the way of Baron R**'s succession, and it is important to bear this in mind in considering, as we are now about to do, the various circumstances attendant on the death of that gentleman.

The chain of evidence on which hangs, as I have so often said, the sole hypothesis by which I can account for the mysterious occurrences that form the subject of our enquiry, is not only of a purely circumstantial character, but also of a nature at once so delicate and so complicated that the failure of a single link would render the remainder altogether worthless.   Unless the case can be made to stand out, step by step, in all its details, from the commencement to the end, its isolated portions become at once a mere chaos of coincidences, singular indeed in many respects, but not necessarily involving any considerable element of suspicion.   It is for this reason that I have, as before stated, endeavoured to lay before you in a distinct and separate form, each particular portion of the subject.   Hitherto our attention has been entirely occupied with the death of Mrs. Anderton, and with various attendant circumstances, the bearing of which upon that occurrence will be more clearly shown hereafter.   We have now to consider the very singular circumstances attending the lapse of the second life— that of Mr. Anderton—intervening, as we have seen, between Mr. Bolton's legacy and Madame R**.

For the purposes of this inquiry, I propose adducing pretty much the same evidence as that given at the inquests held on the bodies of Mrs. and Mr. Anderton.   The final result of the former of these inquests was, as you are aware, a verdict of " Died from natural causes," though the case was at first adjourned for a fortnight in order to admit of a more searching examination of the body, during which time Mr. Anderton remained in custody in his own house.   In the latter case the jury, after some hesitation, returned a verdict of " Temporary insanity, brought on by extreme distress of mind at the death of his wife, and suspicions respecting it which subsequently proved to have been unfounded.".   Our present concern, however, being with the conduct of the Baron rather than that of Mr. Anderton, I have omitted portions not directly bearing upon his part in the matter, and have endeavoured to procure such additions to the evidence of Doctor

Dodsworth and others as might serve to further elucidate the subject of our inquiry.

I now therefore lay before you this portion of the case with especial reference to its bearing upon the proceedings of Baron R★★.

2—*Doctor Dodsworth's Statement.*

I was in attendance on the late Mrs. Anderton during the illness which terminated fatally on the 12th October, 1856. I was first sent for by Mr. Anderton on the night of the 5th of April * in that year. I found her suffering apparently from a slight attack of English cholera, but was unable to ascertain any cause to which it might be attributed. There was nothing to lead to any suspicion of poisoning, indeed this seemed to be rendered almost impossible by the length of time that had elapsed since the last time of taking food and that at which the attack commenced. This was at least three or four hours ; whereas, had the symptoms arisen from the action of any poisonous substance, they would have shown themselves much earlier. This is only my impression from after consideration. No idea of poison occurred to me at the time, nor should I now entertain any were I called in to a similar case. I prescribed the usual remedies for the complaint under which I supposed Mrs. Anderton to be suffering. They appeared to have their effect, though not so rapidly as I should have expected. The symptoms appeared rather to wear themselves out. I visited her several times, as the debility which ensued seemed greater than, under ordinary circumstances, should have followed on such an attack. About a fortnight later she had a fresh seizure, of a very similar kind. This time, however, the symptoms were aggravated, and accompanied by others of a more alarming character. Of these the most conspicuous were nausea, vomiting, violent perspiration, and increasing tendency to diarrhœa. The patient also complained of great sinking of the heart, and of a terrible lowness of spirits, almost amounting to a conviction that death was at hand. In the course of another fortnight or three weeks there was a fresh recurrence of the symptoms. The tongue, which in the former attacks had been clammy and dry, was now covered thickly with dirty mucus, and there was a greatly increased flow of saliva. The condition of the tongue became greatly aggravated as the disease progressed, the mouth and throat becoming ultimately very sore, with great constriction of the latter. The abdomen was distended, and very tender to the touch, the liver also being very full and tender. Pulse low and rapid, decreasing in fullness as the disease progressed, and reaching finally to 130 or 140 ; and the depression of spirits and sinking at the heart considerably increased. The patient appeared to be daily losing strength, and at each attack, which seemed to return periodically at intervals of about a fortnight, the same symptoms appeared more severely than before. Mr. Anderton seemed to be in the deepest distress. From the time when the symptoms first be-

* Compare Section III, 3, etc.

came serious, he hardly ever left her side, administering both food and medicines with his own hand. So far as I am aware, Mrs. Anderton took nothing of any kind from any other person throughout the greater portion of her illness. I have heard her say this herself, in his presence, shortly before her death. For the last few weeks she took scarcely any nourishment, and could with difficulty swallow her medicine. The principal cause of this difficulty lay in the extreme nausea which followed any attempt to swallow, but it was greatly increased by the painful and constricted state of the throat, which was extremely rough and raw, and rendered swallowing very painful. As the disease progressed the vomited matter became strongly coloured with bile, and was of a strong yellow colour. The oppression on the heart also increased, until at length respiration was almost impeded. The heart and pulses also gradually lost power, and latterly the lower portion of the body was almost paralysed, the limbs being stiff, and the whole frame, from the waist downward, very heavy and cold. The patient also suffered from severe cold perspirations, as well as from heat and irritation of the upper portion of the body, and from entire inability to sleep. A very remarkable feature in the case was, that notwithstanding this general sleeplessness, each fresh attack of the malady was preceded by a sound slumber of some hours duration, from which she appeared to be aroused by the return of the more active symptoms of the disorder. ʼI tried all the usual remedies indicated by such symptoms, but without any permanent effect, and I was a good deal perplexed by the anomalous appearance of the case, and especially by its intermittent character, the symptoms recurring, as I have said, with increased severity at regular intervals of about a fortnight. I mentioned my difficulty to Mr. Anderton, and asked if he would wish further advice. At his urgent request I consented, though with some hesitation, to meet Baron R**, who holds, as I was given to understand, a regular diploma from several of the foreign Universities, but whose practice has been of a somewhat irregular character. I first consulted with him on the 12th July.*

(Dr. Dodsworth here details at some length how he became convinced of the Baron's great skill and knowledge of chemistry, and was finally persuaded to meet him in consultation.)

After examination of the patient, however, and some conversation as to the nature of the symptoms and of the remedies employed, I had some difficulty in drawing from him (the Baron) any expression of opinion. He appeared, however, to agree entirely in the course hitherto pursued, and after some further conversation we separated. The consultation took place in Mrs. Anderton's dressing-room, and in passing by the wash-stand on his way out, the Baron suddenly took up a small bottle which was standing there, and turning sharply upon me, asked " if I had tried that ? " On taking it from his hand, I found that it contained tincture of tannin, a preparation much used for the teeth. I was

* Vide Section V., 5.

somewhat startled by the suddenness of the question, and replied in the negative, on which the subject dropped. On my way home, however, I was again struck by the peculiarity of the Baron's manner in putting the question; and on thinking the matter over, the idea suddenly flashed across me that tannic acid was the antidote to antimony, and that the symptoms of poisoning by tartarised antimony, to which attention had just been drawn by Professor Taylor, in the case of the Rugely murder, closely resembled in many respects those under which Mrs. Anderton was then suffering. At the first moment this supposition seemed to account for all the mysterious part of the case; but on reflection the difficulty returned, for it seemed impossible that the poison could have been administered by anyone but Mr. Anderton himself, and I felt it still more impossible to suspect him of such an act, in face of the evident and extreme affection existing between them. On mature reflection, however, I determined on trying, at all events for a time, the course suggested by the Baron, and accordingly exhibited large doses of Peruvian bark, together with other medicines of the same kind. My suspicions were at first increased by the improvement apparently effected by these remedies, and I took occasion to ask Mr. Anderton, in a casual way, in presence of the nurse and one of the servants, whether he had any emetic tartar or antimonial wine in the house. The manner of his reply entirely removed from my mind any idea that either of those present at least had any knowledge of such an attempt as seemed implied by the Baron, and on seeing that gentleman a day or two after, I questioned him as to the true bearing of his suggestion. He disclaimed, however, any such meaning as I had been disposed to attribute to his words, stating, in a general way, that he had before known great benefit to accrue from the exhibition of such medicines in similar cases, and expressing a hope that they might be successful in the present instance. Something, however, in his manner, and especially the great stress laid upon careful watching of the patient's diet while under this course of treatment, led me still to fancy that he was not so entirely without doubt as he wished me to believe; but that, on the contrary, his suspicions pointed towards Mr. Anderton, his friendship for whom made him desirous of concealing them. This opinion was confirmed by the recollection of another apparent instance of suspicion on the part of the Baron, to which, a few days previously, however, I had not at the time attached any importance. I accordingly continued the bark treatment, determining, should any fresh attack occur, to take measures for investigating the matter; for which purpose I gave private orders to the nurse, on whom I knew that I could thoroughly depend, to allow nothing to be removed from the room until I had myself seen the patient. The beneficial effects of the bark continued for about ten or twelve days, at the end of which period I was sent for hurriedly in the middle of the night, the disease having returned with greater violence than at any previous attack. Having done what was in my power to alleviate the immediate pressure of the symptoms, I took an opportunity of privately securing portions of the vomited and other matters, which I immediately had subjected to a searching chemical analysis. No trace, however, of antimony, arsenic, or any similar poison, could be detected, and as the tannic acid appeared now to have lost its remedial power, I came finally to the conclusion that its apparent efficacy had been due to some other unknown cause, and that the suspicions of the Baron were altogether without foundation. I continued the former treatment, varied from time to time as experience suggested, but without being able to arrest the progress of the disease, which I am inclined to think must have been constitutional in its character, and probably hereditary, as I learned from Mr. Anderton that the patient's mother had also died of some internal disease, the exact symptoms of which, however, he was unable to call to mind. Towards the close of the case the patient was almost constantly delirious from debility, and the immediate cause of death was entire prostration and exhaustion of the system. I wished Mr. Anderton to allow a *post mortem* examination, with a view to discovering the true nature of the disorder, but he seemed so extremely sensitive on the subject, and was in such a state of nervous depression, that I forebore to press the point. The Baron also seemed to discourage him from such an idea. Subsequently an order came for an inquest, and I then assisted at the analysis which followed, and which was performed by Mr. Prendergast. We found no traces of antimony in any part of the body or its contents. The report of Mr. Prendergast, in which I fully concurred, will show the result of the analysis. Looking at that, and at all the circumstances of the case,—I was and still am, convinced that Mr. Anderton was perfectly innocent of the crime imputed.

In answer to the queries forwarded at various times by Mr. Henderson, Dr. Dodsworth gives the following replies :

1. In questioning the Baron as to his suggestion respecting the tincture of tannin, I put it plainly to him whether he had been led to make it, by any suspicion of poison. This he disclaimed with equal directness, but with such hestitation as convinced me that the suspicion was really in his mind.

2. I told the Baron that I had exhibited bark and other remedies, and with what success. He smiled, and turned the conversation.

3. The Baron was not present at the *post mortem* examination. He wished very much to be so, but Mr. Prendergast objected so strongly that I was obliged to refuse him. I promised, however, to let him know by telegraph the result of the examination, which took place at Birmingham, where Mr. Prendergast was living at the time. I enclose a copy of the message sent. He offered to assist in removing the intestines, etc., from the body, but this I also declined, as Mr. Prendergast had particularly requested me to allow no one to come near the body after it was opened but myself and some student or surgeon from one of the great hospitals, to render such assistance as might be

necessary. The caution was, I think, a very reasonable one, and I followed it out strictly.

4. The Baron certainly seemed at first, as I thought, annoyed at being excluded, but I attributed this to his interest in the case. He did not make the request as to telegraphing at the time, but wrote to me afterwards on the subject.

5. The object of Mr. Prendergast's precaution was, of course, to prevent the body from being tampered with.

6. By tampered with I mean in such manner as to destroy the traces of the poison.

7. It would, of course, be possible to manufacture traces of poison where none had previously existed, but this could only be done with the view of fastening on an innocent person the guilt of a murder which had never been committed, and was by no means what we intended to guard against in the exclusion of his friends.

8. Certainly had such a thing been successfully attempted in this instance, it would have rendered the case conclusive against Mr. Anderton.

9. The other incident to which I have alluded as evincing suspicion on the part of the Baron, was as follows. We were one morning in consultation in Mr. Anderton's room. I wished to seal a letter. The Baron lighted a taper for me with a piece of paper which he took from the waste basket. As he did so, he appeared struck with something on the paper, and untwisted it and showed it to me. There were only a few letters on it, part having been torn off and part burned. The letters were . . . RTAR EME . . . and part of what was evidently a T. Beneath was the upper portion of a capital P in writing. I did not, however, take much notice of it, and the thing passed from my mind.

10. I have no doubt myself that the paper came from the waste basket. The Baron said so. I did not actually see him take it out, but I saw him stoop to do so. There was nothing physically impossible in his having taken the paper from his own pocket, but I cannot see the slightest reason for such a supposition. The only object he could possibly have had in such an act would have been that of throwing suspicion on Mr. Anderton, and his whole desire evidently was to conceal the suspicions in his own mind as far as possible.

11. The Baron gave me no other grounds for supposing that he suspected anything. On the contrary, he was continually pointing out to me the affection of Mr. Anderton for his wife, and especially the assiduity of his attendance in permitting no one else to administer either food or medicine.

12. The practical effect of all this was certainly, I admit, to impress upon my own mind the suspicious circumstances of the case more strongly perhaps than if they had been pointed out in a directly hostile manner. It is impossible, however, that the Baron could have reckoned upon this, and I feel bound to add that it seems to me exceeding the limits of legitimate inquiry to suggest anything of the kind.

3—*Statement of Mrs. Edwards.*

I am a sick nurse. I was in attendance on poor Mrs. Anderton all through her sickness. The poor lady was greatly cast down. She was expecting her death for weeks before it came. She seemed to think that there was a doom on her. I do not think that she had any suspicion that she was being poisoned. I am sure poor dear lady, no one would ever think of poisoning her, everybody loved her too much. Mr. Anderton was dotingly fond of her. I never saw so good a husband in my life. I could have done anything for him, he was so good to his poor wife. I don't think he hardly ever left her. I used to be vexed sometimes because I said he would not let me do anything for her. I mean he would not let me give her her slops or her physic. She took nothing but slops the best part of the time. She couldn't feel to relish anything at all, and meat made her vomit. For the last two months or better I don't think she took anything from anybody, excepting it was from Mr. Anderton himself. He used to bring her her physic as regular as the clock struck, and everything from the kitchen was took first into his room if he wasn't with the mistress, and he would carry it to her himself. He used to have rare work sometimes to get her to take anything. I am sure she wouldn't have done it poor lady for any but him. Not the last few weeks. She was so very sick and ill, and everything seemed to turn upon her stomach. Mr. Anderton always slept upon a mattress in the mistress's room so as to be within call. The mattress was put upon the floor by the side of the bed, and nobody could have got to the bed without waking him. He was a very light sleeper. The least little sound used to wake him, and I often told him he was going the way to kill himself, and then what would our poor lady do. Once or twice I persuaded him to go out for a bit, and then he always insisted on my not leaving the room while he was away. Even when he was in his study he always made me stay with the lady, and if I wanted to go out for anything, I was to ring for him. Mrs. Anderton was never left without one or other of us for an hour until the last six weeks, when she grew so bad, another nurse had to be got. Then we three did the same way between us. We were obliged to take her because I was getting quite knocked up. How ever Mr. Anderton kept up the way he did, I cannot think or say, but he broke down altogether when the mistress died. I don't think after that the poor gentleman was ever quite right in his head. I remember the doctor asking him one day whether he had any tartar emetic in the house. He said no, but he would get some if it was wanted. Nothing more passed at the time, so far as I know. It was brought to my mind again by something which happened after the poor lady's death. It was nothing very particular, only I found in her room a piece of paper with " Tartar Emetic " printed on it. That was all that was printed, but the word " Poison " was written under it. I kept the paper and showed it to the Baron. I don't know why I did so ; I suppose because he was in the house at the time. Afterwards I showed it to the lawyer, and he took charge of it. I had no particular suspicion, none at all. I can't tell why I took it up. I did it without thinking, quite promiscuous like. I didn't show it to master because he was too ill to be worried. That was the only reason.

The above is the evidence I gave at the inquest. I have nothing more to add. I am quite sure that Mr. and Mrs. Anderton were very fond of each other. I never saw two people so affectionate like. The Baron was very fond of both of them. I don't think Mrs. Anderton liked him much. She seemed to have a sort of dread of him. I don't know why; she never said so. The Baron often used to call on Mr. Anderton, to see the doctor, but, so far as I know, he only saw the mistress once. I think he knew she did not like him, and kept away on purpose. He was a very kind-hearted gentleman. He was always particularly polite and civil-spoken to me. He used often to talk to me about master doting so on mistress. He used to speak about his always giving her her physic and things. I remember one day his saying it wouldn't be very easy to give her anything unwholesome without his knowing of it, or something of that sort. He seemed as if he could never say enough in praise of master, and I am sure he deserved it. I took him the paper I found just like I might have taken it to master if he had been well enough. He was in the house at the time. He had been in the poor lady's room with Dr. Dodsworth just before, and had stayed in the parlour to write something. He sent me into the room to see if he had left his glove there. It was in looking for it that I saw the paper. It was lying just under the bed when I stooped down to look for the glove. I took it up at first, thinking how careless it was to have left it there when the room was put straight after the poor lady died, and then I saw what was written on it. The glove was lying on the floor close to it. There was no vallance to the bed, it had been taken off for the sake of sweetness. I forget exactly what the Baron said when I showed him the paper. It was something that made me think I might get into trouble about it. That was why I showed it to the lawyer. My brother had been to him once before about some money that ought to have come to us. He took the paper to the magistrates, and that was how the inquest came about. I was very angry about it, and so was the Baron. He asked me how I could have been so foolish. I don't know what made me think of taking it to him. I think it was something the Baron said. He did not advise me to do it. He did not advise me anything, but I think he wanted me to burn it. I offered it to him, but he said he was afraid, or something of that kind, and I think that was what put it into my head to ask the lawyer about it.

4—*Memorandum by Mr. Henderson.*

The statement of the other nurse, herewith enclosed, merely corroborates that of Mrs. Edwards, with respect to such matters as

came within her cognisance.   I have therefore not thought it necessary
to insert it here.

Mr. Prendergast's report, also enclosed, is somewhat lengthy, and of a
purely technical character.   It is to the following effect :

1. That, on examination, the body of the late Mrs. Anderton
presented in all respects the precise appearance which would be
exhibited in a case of poisoning by antimony.

2. It was nevertheless possible to account for these appearances,
as the result of chronic *gastritis,* or *gastro enteritis,* though in some
respects not such as either of those diseases would be expected to
present.

3. The strictest and most thorough examination entirely failed to
show the very slightest trace of either antimony or arsenic ; either in
the contents of the various organs, or in the tissues.

4. A portion of the medicine last taken by the deceased was also
examined, but equally without results.

5. From the lengthened period over which the poisoning, if any,
must have extended, and the small doses in which it must have been
administered, it is scarcely possible but that, had such really been the
case, some trace of it must have been found in the tissues, though not
perhaps in the contents of the stomach, etc.

6. In a case of poisoning also, the symptoms would have recurred
in their severest form within a short period of taking the food or
medicine in which it had been administered.   In this case, however,
they appear to have uniformly shown themselves at a late period of the
night, and several hours after either food or medicine had been taken.

7. It is therefore concluded that, notwithstanding the suspicious
appearance of the body on dissection, death is to be attributed not to
poison, but to an abnormal form of chronic *gastro enteritis,* for the
peculiar symptoms of which the exceptional constitution of the deceased may in some degree account.

5—*Statement of Police-Sergeant Reading.*

I am a sergeant on the detective staff of the Metropolitan Police.   In
October, 1856, I was on duty at Notting Hill.   I was employed to
watch a gentleman by the name of Anderton.   He was in custody on
a coroner's warrant for the murder of his lady, but couldn't be removed
on account of being ill.   I was put in the house to prevent his escape.
I did not stay in his room.   I did at first, but it seemed of no use ; so
I spoke to our superintendent, and got leave from him to stop in the
outer-room.   I did this to make things pleasant. I always try to make
things as pleasant as I can, compatible with duty, specially when it's
a gentleman. ° It comes harder on them than on the regular hands,
because they are not so much used to it.   In this case the prisoner
seemed to take on terribly.   He was very weak and ill—too weak
seemingly to get out of bed.   He used to lie with his eyes fixed upon

one corner of the room, muttering sometimes to himself, but I couldn't tell what. He never spoke to anyone. The only time he spoke was once, to ask me to let him see the body. I hadn't the heart to say no ; but I went with him, and kept at the door. He could hardly totter along, he was so weakly. After about half an hour, I thought it was all very quiet, and looked in. He was lying on the floor in a dead faint, and I carried him back. He never spoke again, but lay just as I have said. Of course I took every precaution. Prisoner's room had two doors, one opening on the landing, and the other into the room where I stopped. I locked up the outer-door and put three or four screws into it from the outside. The window was too high to break out at, but our men used to keep an eye on it from the street. At night I used to lock the door of my room and stick open the door between the two. I was relieved occasionally by Sergeant Walsh,* but I mostly preferred seeing to it myself. I like to keep my own work in my own hands, and this was a very interesting case. When I first took charge I made a careful examination of the premises and of all papers, and the like. I found nothing to criminate the prisoner. I found a journal of the lady who was murdered, with a note at the end in his hand-writing ; but so far as it went they seemed to be on very good terms. I found also a lot of prescriptions and notes referring to her illness, but no papers like that found by the nurse, nor any traces of powders or drugs of any kind. I went with the nurse into the bedroom of the murdered party, and made her point out the exact spot where the paper was found. According to what she said it was lying just under the bed on the right-hand side. The glove was lying close to it, but not under the bed. Somehow I didn't quite feel as if it was all on the square. I thought the business of the paper looked rather queer. It didn't seem quite feasible like. I have known a thing of that sort by way of a plant before now, so I thought I'd just go on asking questions. That's always my way. I ask all kinds of questions about everything, feeling my way like. I generally find something turn up that way before I have done. Something turned up this time. I don't know that it was much— perhaps not. I have my own opinion about that. This is how it was. After more questions of one kind and another, I got to something that led me to ask the nurse which side of the bed Mr. Anderton usually went to give the lady food and physic. She and the other servants all agreed that, being naturally left-handed, like, he always went to the *left* hand side of the bed, so as he could get to feed her with a spoon. He was very bad with his right hand. Couldn't handle a spoon with it no more than some of us would with the left. Nurse said she had seen him try once or twice, which he always spilled everything. I mean of course with his right hand. He was handy enough with his left. When I heard this I began to suspect we might be on a false scent. This is the way I looked at it. The glove, as I told you, was

* The evidence of Sergeant Walsh is enclosed, but is merely corroborative of the present statement.—R.H.

lying on the floor by the right side of the bed, so as anybody who dropped it must have been standing on that side which it's the natural side to go to as being nearest the door. The paper was close to it, just under the same side of the bed. Now I took it as pretty clear the prisoner hadn't put the paper there for the purpose, but if he'd done it at all, he had dropped it by accident in giving the stuff. I fancy, too, he'd naturally be particularly careful in giving that sort of stuff not to spill it about the place, so he'd be pretty well sure to take his best hand to it. In that case he'd have dropped it on the left hand side of the bed—not the right. Still, of course, it might have got blown across, or, for the matter of that, kicked, though that was not very likely, as the bed was a wide one, and put in a sort of recess like, quite out of any sort of draught. So I thought I'd have another look at the place, and, poking about under the bed, I found a long narrow box, which the servants told me was full of bows and arrows, and hadn't been moved out of its place since they first came to the house. It took up the whole length of the bed within a foot or so, and lay right along the middle on the floor. There was a mark along the floor that showed how long it had been there. A bit of paper like that could never have got blown right over that without touching it if there had been ever such a draught. When I'd got so far, I fancied things began to look very queer, so I got the bed shifted out of its place altogether. The coffin was in the way, and I got that moved to one side of the room, and pulled the bed right clear of the box. As we shifted the coffin I thought I saw some thing like a piece of paper under the flannel shroud. I said nothing at the time, but waited until the undertaker's men were out of the room and I was alone. I then opened the shroud and found a small folded paper. It was put just under the hands, which were crossed over the bosom of the corpse. I opened it and found a lock of hair, which I saw directly was Mr. Anderton's, and there were a few words in writing which I copied down in my notebook, and then I put the hair and the paper and all back where I found them. The writing was : " Pray for me, darling, pray for me." I knew the hand at once for Mr. Anderton's. His writing is very remarkable, by reason, I suppose, of being so left-handed. Of course that wasn't evidence, but somehow I got an idea out of it that a man wouldn't go on in that way with his wife just after he'd been and murdered her. It struck me that that would be against nature, leastways if he was in his right mind. After I had finished with the coffin I took a look at the box. As I expected, the top was covered ever so thick with dust, and it was pretty clear that, at all events, the bit of paper had never lain atop of it. I put a piece just like it on to try and blew it off again, and it made a great mark and got all dirty. The paper picked up by the nurse was quite clean, or very nearly so. Putting all this together I came pretty nigh a conclusion that, at all events, it wasn't Mr. Anderton as had dropped the paper there. The sides of the box were also dusty, but there were marks on them like as if a brush or a broom had brushed against them. I put the box and the bed back into their places, and went down to question the housemaid.* I found that she had put the room tidy the day Mrs. Anderton died, and had passed a short hair-broom under the bed as there were several things lying about. She said she was quite sure there was no bit of paper there then, as she had stooped down and looked under. I tried with the same broom, and you couldn't reach the box without stooping, as she said. I then inquired who had been in the room between the time of the death and the finding of the paper. No one had been there but the nurse, the doctor, the housemaid, and Baron R**. I was determined to hunt it out if possible. I questioned the nurse and the housemaid—on the quiet, not to excite suspicion—but felt pretty clear they knew nothing more about it; and when next Baron R** came I sounded him about different points. He did not seem to know that Mr. Anderton was so left-handed, nor could I get any information from him on the subject. He didn't seem at first to see what I was driving at, and, of course, I didn't mean he should, but after a while I saw he had struck out the same idea as I had about the place where the paper was found, though I had not meant to let him in to that. He seemed quite struck of a heap by it. I fancied at the moment that he turned regularly pale, but he was just blowing his nose with a large yellow silk handkerchief, and I could not be sure. He said nothing to me of what he had guessed, nor did I to him. I like to keep those things as quiet as I can, particularly from parties' friends. I have not been able to get any further clue, but I am convinced that something is to be made out of that paper business yet. I generally know a scent when I get on one, and my notion is that I am on one now. I did not see the Baron again till the evening before Mr. Anderton made away with himself. He came in then in a great hurry, and insisted on seeing the prisoner. I said I would ask, but did not expect he could, as Mr. Anderton would see or speak to no one. He seemed to be in a sad state, partly with exhaustion after waiting on his wife so long, and partly with the worry of this hanging over him. He was a very sensitive gentleman, and seemed to take it more to heart than any one I ever saw. He wouldn't see any one, even his lawyer. When I told him about the Baron, however, he said he might come in, and they were together half an hour or more. I did not hear anything that passed. When the Baron came out he took me on one side and told me everything was all right, and his friend was sure to get off. He said he was quite overpowered by the good news, and particularly begged that he might not be disturbed by any one, as he thought he could sleep now. He had hardly slept a wink all the time. I promised not to disturb him, and he lay quite quiet all night. I peeped in once or twice to make sure he was there, but did not speak. I noticed a faint smell like peaches once, but did not think anything of it. In the morning I went in to take him his breakfast, and found him dead and quite cold. In his hand was a little bottle

*The housemaid's deposition corroborates this part of the evidence.

which had contained prussic acid, and which had evidently come out of a pocket medicine chest that lay on the bed. I gave the alarm, and the divisional surgeon was sent for, but he was stone dead. At about nine o'clock the Baron's servant came round to know whether he had left a pocket medicine chest the night before. I questioned the servant, and found the Baron had given him a list of the places where he had been, and that he had asked at several already. The medicine chest wanted, proved to be the one found in Mr. Anderton's room. On the pillow I found also a piece of paper in Mr. Anderton's handwriting, of which I enclose a copy.

6—*Pencil note found on the pillow of Mr. Anderton.*

Let no man condemn me for what I do. God knows how I have fought against it. My darling! my own darling! have I not seen you night and day by my side beckoning me to come? Not while a chance remained. Not while there was one hope left to escape this doom of hideous disgrace which dogs me to the death. No, darling, my honour—*your husband's* honour before all. It is over now. No chance—no hope—only ignominy, shame, death. I come, darling. *You* know whether I am guilty of this horrible charge. My darling—my own darling—I see you smile at the very thought. God bless you for that smile. God pardon me for what I am about to do. God reunite us, darling.

SECTION VII

1—*Statement of Mr. Henderson.*

In the concluding portion of the evidence we have now a double object in view. First, to lay before you the various links by which the circumstances, already detailed, are connected into a single chain; and, secondly, to elucidate the general bearing of the whole upon the particular case of the death of Madame R**, into which it is my more immediate duty to inquire. It was this apparent connection with the entire story which first led me to investigate matters otherwise quite beyond my province, and you will, I have no doubt, after reading the evidence, concur in the propriety of my so doing.

It is unfortunate that, in this important part of the case, as previously with regard to the no less important point of the suspicious circumstances attendant on Madame R**'s first illness at Bognor, the evidence of the principal witness is open to very grave question. It is not indeed, as then, that the moral character of the individuals themselves rests under any suspicion, for, so far as I have been able to learn, both the servant-of-all-work, and her lover, John Styles, are perfectly respectable people; whilst the young man Aldridge, though certainly a foolish and perhaps rather a dissipated young fellow, has a very fair character from the house of business in which he is now employed. But the evidence of the two former is, as will be seen, greatly diminished in value by the circumstances under which it was obtained, whilst, in the latter, there is so clear a suspicion of *animus* as cannot but throw still greater doubts upon evidence in itself sufficiently questionable— and rendered yet more so by other circumstances which will hereafter more fully appear.

It was this man Aldridge, whose letter, as you will remember, led to the investigation, of which the result is now before you ; and his statement hereto annexed, that first gave substance to the suspicions of foul play on the part of the Baron, and, in conjunction with the discovery of the enclosed papers, subsequently induced me to extend my inquiries to the cases of Mr. and Mrs. Anderton. I confess that, notwithstanding the doubt with which his statement is surrounded, I am still inclined to accept it as substantially true, though possibly somewhat coloured by personal feeling against the Baron. The point, however, has seemed to me of sufficient importance to justify the occupying a considerable portion of this present division of the case with which such evidence as I have been able to gather respecting the circumstances of his final ejectment, and it will be for you to determine between the story as told by himself and that of Baron R**.

With regard to the other two witnesses who, by one of those singular coincidences that, in criminal cases, seem so often to occur, are able to confirm in some degree the evidence of Aldridge, there is, I think, less difficulty. They had certainly no business where they were, but the circumstances are such as to fully acquit them of any felonious intent, while even had such existed, it would be difficult to see how the fact of such intent could have exercised any influence over their present statements. It is moreover quite clear that there has been no collusion upon the subject.

I have now only to refer, in conclusion, to the fragment of paper found in the Baron's rooms in Russell Place, and the marked copy of the " Zoist," belonging to the late Mr. Anderton, to which Mr. Morton referred in his statement* as having formed the subject of discussion at Mr. Anderton's house on the evening of the 13th of October, 1854. The first of these is a portion of a letter, which I have endeavoured, so far as possible, to complete. Admitting that I have done so correctly, and coupling it with the fact of the visit which, as I have been able to ascertain, was paid by a foreign lady to the Baron " very early in the morning " following the death of Madame R**, it appears to throw no inconsiderable light upon the extraordinary circumstances of the death of Madame R**. The bearing of the latter upon the case will be perhaps less clear. I have no hesitation in admitting that when the connection first suggested itself to my own mind, I at once dismissed it as too absurd to be entertained for a moment. But I feel bound to add that the further my inquiries have progressed, the more strongly

* Section II, 2.

this apparent connection has forced itself upon me as the only clue to a maze of coincidences such as it has never before been my lot to encounter, and that while even now unable to accept it as a fact, I find it still more impossible to thrust it altogether on one side. I have therefore left the matter for your decision, merely pointing out, as I have before, in the opening portion of my report, that, even admitting the influence of these passages upon the mind of the Baron, and the ultimate success of the plan founded upon their suggestion, that success, however extraordinary, may not necessarily involve, as at first appears, the admission of those monstrous assertions of the " mesmeric " journal on which it was based.

With these observations, I now submit to your consideration the concluding portion of the evidence, after which it will only be necessary for me to take a brief review of the whole case before leaving it finally in your hands.

2—*Statement of Mrs. Jackson.*

My name is Mary Jackson. I live in Goswell Street, City Road. I am a monthly and sick-nurse. In June, 1856, I was engaged to nurse Madame R**. I was recommended to the Baron by Dr. Marsden, who lodged in the same house. I have often nursed for him. Madame R** was not very ill. I don't think she was ill enough to require a nurse. Of course she was the better for one—everybody always is—but she could have done without one. I came by the Baron's wish. He was anxious like. The poor gentleman was very fond of his wife. I never saw such a good husband. I am sure no other husband would have done what he did, and she so cold to him. I don't think she cared about him at all. She hardly ever spoke to him unless it was when he spoke first. She never spoke much. She always seemed frightened ; especially when the Baron was there. She certainly seemed to be afraid of him, but I can't tell why. He was always kind to her. He was the nicest and most civil-spoken gentleman I ever knew. It was not that he was not particular. Quite the reverse. I wish all husbands were half so particular, and then nurses wouldn't so often get into trouble. Everything used to be done like clockwork. Every morning he used to give me a paper what was to be given in the day. I mean medicine and food. A list of everything with the time it was to be taken. Everything used to be ready, and I used it give it regular. No one else ever used to give anything. *The Baron never gave anything himself.* Never at all. I am quite sure of that. He used to say that it was nurse's business, and so it is. He often said he had seen so much sickness he had learned never to interfere with the nurse, and I only wish all other gentlemen would do the same. He used to be very particular about the physic. We always have the bottles for our perquisite. We get a shilling a dozen for them all round if they are clean. The Baron objected to this. He allowed me a shilling a dozen instead. The bottles were all put away in a cupboard. They never used to be quite emptied. The Baron always made a point of having fresh in before the old was quite finished He said he always liked to have them to refer to in case of accident or mistake. He was a very careful gentleman. I nursed Madame R** every day until her recovery. I am quite certain that, during the hours I was there, nothing was ever given to her but what passed through my hands.

3—*Statement of Mrs. Ellis.*

My name is Jane Ellis. I am a sick-nurse, and live in Goodge Street, Tottenham Court Road. In about the end of July, 1856, I was engaged as night nurse to Madame R**. Perhaps she did not exactly require one. She was ill, but she could help herself. At times she was very ill. It was much more comfortable for her, and she could afford it. Baron R** never seemed to spare anything for her. She was generally worst at night. The worst attacks used to come on about every fort-night. It was generally on a Saturday. I took turn and turn about with Mrs. Jackson. She took the day work, and I took the night. I used to come at ten o'clock, and leave at breakfast time. During that time I was never out of the room. It was the Baron's particular desire. When I first came he made it a condition that I should never leave the room, and never go to sleep. He was the most particular gentleman I ever nursed for. I have nothing whatever to say against him. Quite the contrary. He was always civil and pleasant spoken, and behaved most handsome, as a gentleman should do. He was un-common fond of the lady. She didn't seem to care much about him. She was ill, poor soul, and could not care about anybody. She seemed quite frightened like. When the Baron came into the room she used to follow him about with her eyes, as if she was afraid of him. I never heard him say an unkind word. Other times she would lie quite quiet, and not speak a word for hours. She seemed afraid of everybody. If I moved about the room, I could see her eyes following me about and watching me everywhere. I think it was part of her complaint. The Baron was most attentive. I never saw such an attentive husband. He used to lie in the next room. It opened into the bedroom, and he always had the door wide open. He was a wonderfully light sleeper. If either of us spoke a word, he would be in the room directly, to ask what was the matter. I couldn't even move across the room but what he would hear it. He was a wonderful man. He seemed to live almost without sleep. I think it must have been the meat did it. He used to eat enormous quantities of meat. I never saw a man eat so much. When I first came he used to joke with me about it. Madame R** was not so bad then, and we used to talk sometimes. He told me it was because he was a mesmeriser. I don't believe in mesmerism. I told him so. He didn't say anything;

he only laughed.   One night he offered to send me to sleep.   That was when I had been there about a week.   I said he might try if he could. He looked hard at me, ever so long, and made some odd motions with his hands.   I did go to sleep.   I don't believe it was mesmerism.   Of course not.   I think it was looking at his eyes.   I told him so.   He asked if he should do it again.   He did it once more.   That was the night after.   I went to sleep then almost directly.   Of course I knew it was not mesmerism, but I couldn't help it.   He did not talk about it any more.   He only said that I must take care not to go to sleep of my own accord.   I did drop asleep three or four times after that.   That was not from anything the Baron did.   He was not in the room at the time. He must have been in the next room.   I suppose the door was open. It always was.   The first time I went to sleep was about a week after we had talked about the mesmerism.   It was on a Saturday night, or Friday.   I am not quite sure which.   It was one of the nights when Madame R** was so ill.   She had gone to sleep at about eleven o'clock. She seemed very well then.   She was sleeping quite quiet.   I suppose I must have dropped off.   I was awoke by her moaning in her sleep. That was about one o'clock.   She soon woke up in great pain, and had a very bad attack.   The Baron came into the room just as I awoke. Something woke him, and he came in directly.   He told me what it was that woke him.   It was me snoring.   He said so.   I fell asleep again a fortnight after in the same way.   The Baron was not there. Madame R** was asleep.   She had not slept for many nights.   I must have dropped off in a doze hearing her so nicely asleep.   The Baron woke me.   That was at about one o'clock.   He was very much displeased.   He told me Madame R** had been walking in her sleep and might have killed herself.   He said she went into the kitchen. I am certain that was where he said.   I can swear it.   He asked what I had taken for supper, and tasted what was left of the beer.   He seemed very much vexed and disturbed.   I was very sorry, and promised to be very careful another time.   I never had such a thing happen in any other case, and I told him so.   He said he would look over it that time, but it must never happen again.   He went up-stairs afterwards.   I think it was to speak to somebody.   He said somebody had seen her, I think.   Madame R** was ill that night.   She began to moan while we were talking, and had a very bad attack. The Baron said she must have caught cold, and I am afraid she did. I determined to be particularly careful for the time to come.   I was very careful for some time, particularly when she was asleep.   She hardly slept at all for two weeks, but when she did I was very careful. At the end of that time I must have fallen asleep again.   I was hardly aware of it.   I know I must have been asleep, because when I looked at the clock it was two hours later than I thought.   Madame R** was ill again that night.   I was very much vexed.   I began to think somebody was playing tricks upon me.   It was so strange, coming every fortnight.   I did not tell the Baron.   I know it was wrong, but I was afraid. Next fortnight I was on the look out. Madame R✱✱ went to sleep again. I was determined not to go to sleep. I thought somebody must have played tricks with the beer, so I wouldn't drink it. I ate no supper and drank nothing but some strong green tea I made for myself. I was quite sure the tea must keep me awake. It did not. I awoke with a great start about one o'clock, and found Madame R✱✱ bad again as usual. I was very much bothered about it. I made up my mind to tell the Baron if it happened again. It did happen again, but I did not tell him. Madame R✱✱ was so bad then I was really afraid, and, after that, it never happened again, and she got well. I know I ought to have told the Baron. I am sorry I did not. Such a thing never happened to me before. Of course I have slept in a sick-room before, but not when it was against orders. I was there about three months. I dropped asleep in that way, I think, six times, but I am not quite sure. It was always while Madame R✱✱ was asleep. She was always bad afterwards. I did not say anything to her about it, or about her walking. The Baron particularly desired I would not. He said it would frighten her. He never asked me again whether I had been asleep, or I would have told him. I was really going to tell him once or twice, but something always happened to stop me. I can swear that nothing of the kind ever happened to me before. There must have been something wrong. I have sick-nursed twenty years, and have the best characters from many doctors and patients.✱

4—*Statement of Mr. Westmacott.*

" London, 20th September, 1857.
" Sir,

I have the honour to inform you that in compliance with your request I have submitted to the most careful and searching examination and analysis the contents of three dozen and seven (43) medicine phials forwarded by you for that purpose.

The number and contents of these phials correspond exactly with the prescriptions, &c., furnished by Messrs. Andrews and Empson,† and after the most exact analysis I have been unable to detect the slightest trace of either arsenic, antimony, or any similar substance.

I have the honour to be,
Your most obedient servant,
THOMAS WESTMACOTT,
Analytical Chemist."

5.—*Statement of Henry Aldridge.*

My name is Henry Aldridge. I am a clerk in the employ of Messrs. Simpson and Co., City. In the summer of 1856 I came to lodge at Mrs. Brown's, in Russell Place. I did not come there first as a lodger,

---

✱ This I find to be the case.—R.H.
† The chemists from whom the Baron obtained his medicines.

but as a friend of her son. I had known him in Australia. We were together in the same store in Melbourne, and got to be great friends. We did not come home in the same ship. That is a mistake. I came home some weeks before he did, and was in Liverpool when he arrived. I think he came in the Lightning, but cannot be sure. I used to board so many ships that I can't call to mind. I was in a Liverpool house then for a time, and it was my duty to board every ship as she came up. I agreed to go with him to London. I could not go directly, as I had to give notice to my employers, but I was to follow him. He asked me to stay with him for his wedding at his mother's house, and I did so. That was how I first came to Russell Place. After that he arranged with his mother for me to take a room regularly, and I was to pay so much a week, and so much more when I got a situation. I was not aware of the Baron making any objection. I saw very little of him. I slept on the floor above, and was always very careful not to make any noise on account of Madame R**. She was ill, and I took particular care not to disturb her. I used sometimes to be out late. I have been intoxicated in my life. Not very often. Not at all while I was in Russell Place. I have been out to my friends while I was there, and have drunk wine and spirits, but never to be the worse for it. I may have been merry. I don't say I have not been once or twice a little excited with wine. What I mean is, that I have never been in such a state as not to be quite conscious of what I was doing, and quite able to control myself. I am quite certain that I never made the slightest disturbance, or could have done so without knowing it. That I will swear to. I believe the Baron accused me of it to Mrs. Brown. He spoke to her several times about it, and wished her to turn me out. She said she had never seen anything wrong, and couldn't say anything till she did, because I was her son's friend. At last he got her to do it. The reason was that I was found by a policeman on the doorstep at about twelve o'clock one night insensible. The policeman knocked and rang, and woke up the house, and the Baron said I was drunk. I was perfectly sober. I had had nothing whatever but one small bottle of ale. The facts of the case were these, and I will swear to them. I had been kept late at our office with some heavy correspondence, and had then walked home with another clerk from the same office—William Wells —having taken nothing but one small bottle of ale, which I had at a public-house in High Holborn, as I felt quite tired. Wells had some brandy-and-water. He left me at the corner of Tottenham Court Road. When I got to Russell Place I tried to open the door with my latch-key, but the latch was fastened. I then rang at the bell, but could not make it sound, and the handle came out loose as if the wire was broken. I tried the key once more, and was just thinking whether I should not go to some place, as I did not like to disturb Madame R** by knocking, when the door was opened from the inside. I turned round to go in when something was thrust into my face, and I can remember nothing more. I must have fallen down insensible and the policeman found me. This is the truth. I could not see who opened the door. There was a street lamp close to the area gate, but the person was in the shadow. I cannot account for it. I made sure at the time it was a trick of the Baron to get me turned out. I think so still, but am not so sure of it as I was. What I mean is, that, on reflection, I don't think it is certain enough to accuse him of such a thing. I will swear to the truth of what I have said. I will swear that I was perfectly sober—as sober as I am now. My employers and Will Wells can prove it. I do not know why the Baron should have wished so much to turn me out. We never had words about anything. I don't think I ever spoke to him but once. I mean not more than " Good morning," or such like. That was on the occasion about which I wrote to the Assurance Office after Madame R**'s death. It was one Saturday night. I had had a half-holiday, and had been up to Putney in a boat with some friends. We had drunk a good deal of beer and shandy-gaff, but I was not drunk. I was quite sober, though perhaps a little excited. Nothing to speak of. I got home at about eleven o'clock. I had a latch-key then, but the lock was hampered ; and when I got back home I found the servant girl sitting up to let me in. I went up very quietly not to disturb Madame R**. I saw her bedroom-door ajar as I passed. The door of the room next to it was wide open, and there was some sort of lamp burning. No one moved or said anything as I went by. I took off my shoes to go more softly, but the house was old, and it was impossible to move without the stairs creaking a little. The stairs below the Baron's room were stone and did not creak. I had a candle which I shaded carefully with my hand. I went to bed, but I suppose I was over-tired, for I could not get to sleep. The night was very hot. When I had been in bed about a couple of hours I thought I would have a good wash and see if that would cool me. I got up and went to the washhand-stand. I found the jug empty. The maid often forgot to fill it. I took the jug and went out on to the landing to fill it at the tap. I went very softly, not to disturb Madame R**. As I got on to the landing, I saw some one coming out of her room, and went to look over the bannister. From the landing of my room you can see that of the floor below. I looked over, and saw that it was Madame R**. She was in her dressing-gown, but had no candle. She went to the stairs, and there I lost sight of her. As I watched her past the door of the other room, I saw the shadow of a man's head and shoulders upon the wall, as if somebody was watching her. I leaned against the bannister to watch her, and it creaked, and the shadow vanished directly. When I looked up again it was gone, and at first I thought it must have been fancy, but I am quite certain about it now. I was only doubtful for the moment. It was so sudden. I could swear to it now. I saw it perfectly plain. I saw it all the time Madame R** was going down the first flight of stairs About twelve of them. She was at the corner when I turned and leaned over to watch her. I felt convinced that Madame R** was walking in her sleep. The staircase was quite dark beyond the corner, and she had walked straight down. I was afraid she would hurt herself, and went down to the Baron's door. He was asleep; at least I had to knock twice. He then came to the door, and I told him what I had seen. He seemed a good deal annoyed, and at once took up the lamp, and went down stairs. I looked over the bannister, and saw him go down. From that place you can see right down to the door which leads to the kitchen-stairs. There is a glass partition between them and the hall. I saw him go in at the door, and I saw the light through the glass as he went part of the way down stairs. Presently he came up again, and stood back from the door while Madame R** came up past him, and walked up stairs, and he then followed her. When I saw her coming up, I went back to my own landing and looked over. She went back to her own room, fast asleep still, as it seemed to me, and he followed. I heard whispering in the room, and then the Baron came up to me. He thanked me very much for telling him, and said that Madame R** had gone down into the kitchen, and was just coming out as he got to the foot of the stairs. He particularly begged me never to mention it, as it might come to her ears and do her harm, and I have never spoken of it to any one till I wrote to the Assurance Office. I had almost forgotten all about it when it was recalled to my mind by seeing that poor Madame R** had killed herself in a sleep-walking fit. I then wrote. I had no malice against the Baron, nor have I now. I don't know why he tried to turn me out. I suppose he really thought I disturbed his wife. He was very fond of her, and I dare say he was anxious and fretful about her. I was very angry at the time, but when I come to think of it, I dare say I was hard upon him. He never seemed to bear me any grudge about what I had seen. On the contrary, he always said he was very much obliged to me. This is all I know on the subject, and I can swear to the truth of every word. I am quite positive he said Madame R** had been into the kitchen.

6—*Statement of Miles Thompson.*

I am a police constable. In August, 1856, I used to be on night duty in Russell Place. I remember Baron R** speaking to me one night, and asking me to keep a look out as often as I could of a night to keep the street quiet. He gave me five shillings for my extra trouble. I was on the beat one night about twelve o'clock when I saw some one lying on the Baron's door-step. It was a young gentleman, and at first I thought he was dead, but found he was only insensible. I set him up against the railings, and was going to ring the bell, when I saw a latch-key in his hand. I tried it in the door and it opened it directly, and I took him into the hall. I then knocked and rang till somebody came. The bell rang quite well. The Baron came down in his dressing-gown, and two or three other people. I offered to go for a doctor, but the Baron said he was only drunk. I helped to carry him up-stairs, and get him into bed. The Baron gave me half-a-crown for my trouble. He seemed very much annoyed, as was natural, and said he wished I had taken the young man to the station. I think he was drunk myself. He smelt a little of beer, but not much. I helped put him to bed, and went away. That is all I know.

N.B.—By letters from Messrs. Simpson and Mr. Wells, Mr. Aldridge's assertion that he was sober is borne out up to the time of the latter's leaving him at the corner of Tottenham Court Road, certainly not more than half-an-hour before he was found as above stated by Police-contable Thompson.   R.H.

7—*Statement of John Johnson.*

to

mister endusson sir obeadent to yore Comands i hev eksammd tha belwir in russle please wich in my humbel Hopinnium it hev ben Templd wit by sum Hunperfeshnl And wich tha Wir it hev ben tuk hof tha Kranke & putt bak hall nohowlik wich hany Purfeshnl And wud be a Shammd for 2 du It i am sur yore hobeadnt survnt too Comand

jon jonsun

Plommr hand belanger
totunmcort rode
lundon

8—*Statement of Susan Turner.*

My name is Susan Turner. In August, 1856, I was general servant to Mrs. Brown in Russell Place. I remember the night that Madame R** came down-stairs. I had sat up to let Mr. Aldridge in because the latch was broken. Mistress broke it that afternoon. I don't suppose the Baron knew anything about it. Mr. Aldridge came in rather late. I cannot justly say the time. He was quite right. I mean quite sober. He went straight up to bed. I did not go up to bed. My young man was in the kitchen. He is a very respectable young man upon a railway. I don't know what railway. I know he goes to Scotland sometimes with his engine, that is all. He is what they call a fireman. He was going down with a luggage-train some-where that night very late, and came to see me. Mistress didn't know he was there. He came in after she was gone to bed. He was to start at two, and we sat till about one. He was just going away, and we were standing at the kitchen door when we heard somebody in the hall. I said, " Oh, Lor ! that's missis." He said, " She'll be coming to look for you," and wanted me to go and meet her while he cut out by the area. I said no, that wouldn't do, by reason of it being all glass and a gas lamp at top of the area steps.* I pulled him along to the lumber-room. The lumber-room is behind the kitchen and the cellar. There are some old boxes and things there, but nobody ever

* The arrangement alluded to will be seen from the accompanying plan. The inner partition is entirely of glass, while the outer has a row of large panes along the top.

goes into it. I thought my mistress would not think of looking there.
Just as we got to the door we saw somebody come from the hall and
down the stairs. I whispered to John, "Why that's not missis—
that's Madame." My mistress was very tall and stout, and Madame
R** was small and thin. I could see her as she came through the
door, because there was some sort of light in the hall. She came right
down-stairs and past where we were. She went right on into the little
place at the end where the Baron kept all his bottles and stuff. She
did not go into the kitchen. Not at all. I will swear to that. She
went into the Baron's place. The laboratory, I dare say it is; I
don't know. It was where the bottles are. John and me crept to the
window and looked out. The window of the lumber-room looks right
into the window of the back room where the bottles are. You could
see in quite plain. It was a bright moonlight night, and there is a
sort of tin looking-glass over the back room window to make more
light like. We saw Madame go into the room and take a bottle from
a shelf. She poured out a glassful and drank it. Then she put the
bottle back in its place. It was the last in the second shelf. Then
she went out again, and when we turned round we saw a light shining
into the room from the kitchen stairs. It stayed there till Madame
had gone past our door again, and then it went up again. Just as it
got to the top of the stairs I peeped out and saw it was the Baron.
Madame was close behind him. I said to John, "Why, John, there's
the Baron." He said he supposed he had come to look after his wife.
After they had gone John and me went into the bottle place. We
found the glass on the table. There were a few drops of stuff in it.
John and me smelt it, and it was just like wine. It tasted just like
wine, too. Then we looked for the bottle. It was at the end of the
second shelf. It was about half-full of stuff that looked like wine. There
was something in gold letters on the bottle. I can't tell what it was.
It was " vin " something. I know that because John and me settled
it must mean wine. I think I should know the rest if I saw it—[being
here shown several labels, witness picked out the following " Vin. Ant.
Pot. Tart." designating antimonial wine, a mixture of sherry and tartar
emetic]—I am pretty sure that was the one. I remember it because
they were such funny words. I remember John and me joking about
" pots " and " pies." The stuff in the bottle smelt just like wine. It
was just like sherry wine. I did not taste that. John wouldn't let me.
He said I might go and poison myself for aught I knew. We put the
bottle back and then John went away. I said nothing about it to
anybody. Not even when Madame was taken ill that night. I was afraid
by reason of John. I have never said a word about it to any living soul
till I was asked to-day. Certainly not to Mr. Aldridge, nor he to me.
I will swear to the truth of all I have said. I am quite positive that
Madame never went near the kitchen. I am quite positive that the
Baron must have seen her come out of the bottle place. He was standing
with the candle in his hand waiting for her. That I can swear.

N.B.—The statement of the "young man" referred to fully corroborates the above statement. The accompanying plan will make this witness' evidence more clear.

*Plan of basement floor of Baron R**'s lodgings, Russell Place.*

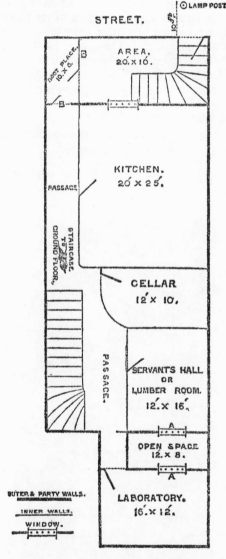

A A Windows of lumber-room and laboratory referred to in the evidence of John Sanders and Mary Allen.
B B Glass Partitions.

9—*Copy of a letter from a leading Mesmerist to the compiler, with reference to the power claimed by mesmeric operators over those subjected to their influence.*

" MY DEAR SIR,—   " *Dorset Square.*

. . . . Many times after throwing Sarah Parsons into the mesmeric state, I have *willed* her to go into a dark room and pick up a pin or other article equally minute, and however powerless she might be at the time out of the state was quite immaterial. My will and power being employed was sufficient. Then, Mr. L——, a paralytic, under my influence, without losing consciousness or undergoing any recognisable change, has many times, with the lame leg, stepped up on to and down again from an ordinary dining-room chair. This of course was a masterpiece of mesmeric manipulation. I wish I could write more and better, but my eyes forbid ＊ ＊ ＊

With kindest regards, Yours most truly,

D. HANDS."

10—*Fragment of a Letter found in the Baron's room after the death of Madame R**.*

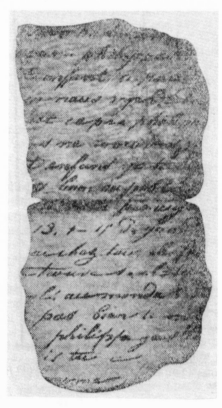

COMPLETED.

........On (?)

te..pendrait n'e..st se pas mon p..auvre philippe ? E..h
bien par ce..t enfant, ce pauvre..petit ange (?) q..ui nous
regarde du..haut du ciel, n'..est ce pas philipp..e et que
no..us ne reverrons ja..mais, par ce..t enfant je te le
j..ure. Tu m'en sa..is bien capable j..e crois. En..core
une fois, aujo..urd'hui c'est le..13, le 15, de grand..matin
je se..rai chez toi ; il fa..ut que je t..e troube seul, tu i .. ne
comprends ; se..ul au monde ! n'..en sais tu..pas bien le
moy..en ? O..h ! philippe je t'ai..me (je t'aime ?) sa..is
tu ce qu..e c'est qu' une f..emme ja..louse ?

Translation of above.

(They) would hang thee, would they not, my poor Philip ? Well,
by that child—that poor (little angel) who is now—is it not so, Philip ?
—looking down on us from heaven, and whom we shall never see again,
by that child I swear it to you. Once more. To-day is the 13th.
On the 15th very early in the morning I shall be at your house. I
must find you alone—you understand me, alone in the world ! Do
you not well know the means ? Oh, Philip, I love thee (I love thee).
Knowest thou what a jealous woman is ?

11—*Extracts from the " Zoist Magazine," No. XLVII., for October,*
1854.
" MESMERIC CURE OF A LADY WHO HAD BEEN TWELVE YEARS IN THE
HORIZONTAL POSITION, WITH EXTREME SUFFERING. By the Rev.
R. A. F. Barrett, B.D., Senior Fellow of King's College, Cambridge.

* * * * *

" In January, 1852, I was calling upon ——, when she happened to
tell me that she had been in considerable pain for a fortnight past;
that the only thing that relieved her was mesmerism ; but the friend
who used to mesmerise her was gone. . . . I continued to mesmerise
her occasionally for some months. . . .
" *April 21st.*—I kept her asleep an hour and a quarter in the morning
and the same in the evening. She said* her throat looked parched and
feverish ; at her request *I ate some black currant paste, which she said
moistened it.* . . . She said, ' Before you ate, my stomach was contracted and had a queer-looking sort of moisture in it; now the
stomach is its full size and does not look shrunk, and part of the
moisture is gone.'
" I. ' But you could not *get nourishment* so ? '
" A. ' Yes : *I could get all my system wants.*'

* * * * *

* In a former portion of the case we are told that this patient was *clairvoyant* and
could see her own internal condition.—R.H.

" *April 26th.*—In the evening I kept her asleep one hour, *and took tea for her.*
" *April 27th.*— . . . I ate dinner and she felt much stronger.

*   *   *   *   *

" I kept her asleep two hours and a quarter in the morning and one hour in the evening, *eating for her as usual.*"

SECTION VIII.   CONCLUSION

THERE now only remains for me, in conclusion, to sum up as briefly and succinctly as possible the evidence contained in the preceding statements.   In so doing, it will be necessary to adopt an arrangement somewhat different from that which has been hitherto followed. Each step of the narrative will therefore be accompanied with a reference to the particular deposition from which it may be taken.

I

First then, for what may be called the preliminary portions of the evidence.   With these we need here deal but very briefly.   They consist almost entirely of letters furnished by the courtesy of a near relation of the late Mrs. Anderton, and read as follows :

Some six or seven and twenty years ago, the mother of Mrs. Anderton —Lady Bolton—after giving birth to twin daughters, under circumstances of a peculiarly exciting and agitating nature, died in child-bed. Both Sir Edward Bolton and herself appear to have been of a nervous temperament, and the effects of these combined influences is shown in the highly nervous and susceptible organisation of the orphan girls, and in a morbid sympathy of constitution, by which each appeared to suffer from any ailment of the other.   This remarkable sympathy is very clearly shown in more than one of the letters I have submitted for your consideration, and I have numerous others in my possession which, should they be considered insufficient, will place the matter, irregular as it certainly is, beyond the reach of doubt.   I must request you to bear it particularly and constantly in mind throughout the case.

Almost from the time of the mother's death, the children were placed in the care of a poor, but respectable woman, at Hastings.   Here the younger, whose constitution appears to have been originally much stronger than that of her sister, seems to have improved rapidly in health, and in so doing to have mastered, in some degree, that morbid sympathy of temperament of which I have spoken, and which in the weaker organisation of her elder sister, still maintained its former ascendency.   They were about six years old when, whether through the carelessness of the nurse or not, is immaterial to us now, the younger was lost during a pleasure excursion in the neighbourhood.   Every inquiry was made, and it appeared pretty clear that she had fallen into the hands of a gang of gipsies, who at that time infested the country round, but no further trace of her was ever after discovered.

The elder sister, now left alone, seems to have been watched with redoubled solicitude. There is nothing, however, in the years immediately following Miss C. Bolton's disappearance having any direct bearing upon our case, and I have, therefore, confined my extracts from the correspondence entrusted to me, to two or three letters from a lady in whose charge she was placed at Hampstead, and one from an old friend of her mother, from which we gather the fact of her marriage. The latter is chiefly notable as pointing out the nervous and highly sensitive temperament of the young lady's husband, the late Mr. Anderton, to which I shall have occasion at a later period of the case, more particularly to direct your attention. The former give evidence of a very importance fact; namely, that of the liability of Miss Bolton to attacks of illness equally unaccountable and unmanageable, bearing a perfect resemblance to those in which she suffered in her younger days sympathetically with the ailments of her sister; and, therefore, to be not improbably attributed to a similar cause.

II

Thus far for the preliminary portion of the evidence. The second division places before us certain peculiarities in the married life of Mrs. Anderton; its more especial object, however, being to elucidate the connection between the parties whose history we have hitherto been tracing, and the Baron R**, with whose proceedings we are properly concerned.

It appears then, that in all respects but one, the married life of Mr. and Mrs. Anderton was particularly happy. Notwithstanding their retired and often somewhat nomad life, and the limits necessarily imposed thereby to the formation of friendships, the evidence of their devoted attachment to each other is perfectly overwhelming. I have no less than thirty-seven letters from various quarters, all speaking more or less strongly upon this point, but I have thought it better to select from the mass a small but sufficient number, than to overload the case with unnecessary repetition. In one respect alone their happiness was incomplete. It was, as had been justly observed by Mrs. Ward, most unfortunate that the choice of Miss Bolton should have fallen upon a gentleman, who however eligible in every other respect, was, from his extreme constitutional nervousness, so peculiarly ill-adapted for union with a lady of such very similar organisation. The connection seems to have borne its natural fruit in the increased delicacy of both parties, their married life being spent in an almost continual search after health. Among the numerous experiments tried with this object, they at length appear to have had recourse to mesmerism, becoming finally patients of Baron R**, a well-known professor of that and other kindred impositions.

Mrs. Anderton had not been long under his care when the remonstrances of several friends led to the cessation of the Baron's immediate manipulations, the mesmeric fluid being now conveyed to the patient through the intervention of a third party. Mademoiselle Rosalie, " the medium " thus employed, was a young person regularly retained by Baron R** for that purpose, and of her it is necessary here to say a few words.

She appears to have been about the age of Mrs. Anderton, though looking perhaps a little older than her years ; slight in figure, with dark hair and eyes, and in all respects but one answering precisely to the description of that lady's lost sister. The single difference alluded to that of wide and clumsy feet, is amply accounted for by the nature of her former avocation. She had been for several years a tight-rope dancer, &c., in the employ of a travelling-circus proprietor ; who, by his own account, had purchased her for a trifling sum, of a gang of gipsies at Lewes, just at the very time when the younger Miss Bolton was stolen at Hastings by a gang whose course was tracked through Lewes to the westward. Of him she was again purchased by the Baron, who appears, even at the outset, to have exercised a singular power over her, the fascination of his glance falling on her whilst engaged upon the stage, having compelled her to stop short in the performance of her part. There can, I think, be little doubt that this girl Rosalie was in fact the lost sister of Mrs. Anderton, and of this we shall find that the Baron R** very shortly became cognisant.

It does not appear that on the first meeting of the sisters he had any idea of the relationship between them. He was, indeed, perfectly ignorant of the early history of both. The extraordinary sympathy therefore which immediately manifested itself between them was not improbably set down by him as a mere result of the mesmeric *rapport*, and it was not till he had been for some weeks in attendance on Mrs. Anderton that accident led him to divine its true origin. Nor, on the other hand, does this singular sympathy—a sympathy manifested in a precisely similar manner to that known to have existed years ago between the sisters—appear to have raised any suspicion of the truth in the mind of either Mrs. Anderton or her husband. From the former, indeed, all mention of her early life had been carefully kept till she had probably almost, if not entirely, forgotten the event, while the latter merely remembered it as a tale which had long since ceased to possess any present interest.

The two sisters were thus for several weeks in the closest contact, the effects of which may or may not have been heightened by the so-called mesmeric connection between them, before any suspicion of their relationship crossed the mind of any one. One evening, how-ever,—and from certain peculiar circumstances we are enabled to fix the date precisely to the 13th of October, 1854,—the Baron appears beyond all doubt to have become cognisant of the fact. I must request your particular attention to the circumstances by which his discovery of it was attended.

On that evening the conversation appears to have very naturally turned upon a certain extraordinary case professed to be reported in a number of the " Zoist Mesmeric Magazine," published a few days before.   The pretended case was that of a lady suffering from some internal disorder which forbade her to swallow any food, and receiving sustenance through mesmeric sympathy with the operator, who " *ate for her*."   From this extraordinary tale the conversation turned naturally to other manifestations of constitutional sympathy, as an instance of which Mr. Anderton related the story of Mrs. Anderton's lost sister, and the singular bond which had existed between them. The conversation appears to have continued for some time, and in the course of it a jesting remark was made by one of the party in allusion to the story of eating by deputy, to which I am inclined to look as the keynote of this horrible affair.

II., 2

" I said," deposes Mr. Morton, " I said *it was lucky for the young woman that the fellow didn't eat anything unwholesome.*"

From the moment these words were spoken the Baron appears to have dropped out of the conversation altogether.   More than this, he was clearly in a condition of great mental pre-occupation and disturbance.   Mr. Morton goes on to describe the singularity of his manner, the letting his cigar expire between his teeth, and the tremulousness of his hands, so excessive, that in attempting to re-light it he only succeeded in destroying that of his friend.   There can, I think, be no doubt whatever that from that moment he believed thoroughly in the identity of Rosalie with the lost sister of Mrs. Anderton.   What other ideas the conversation had suggested to him we must endeavour to ascertain from the evidence that follows.

II., 5

On the morning of the day succeeding that on the evening of which he had become convinced of Rosalie's identity, we find Baron R** at Doctor's Commons inquiring into the particulars of a will by which the sum of 25,000*l*. had been bequeathed, under certain conditions, to the children of Lady Boleton.   Under the provisions of this will, the girl Rosalie was, after her sister and Mr. Anderton, the heir to this legacy.   We need, I think, have no difficulty in connecting the acquisition of this intelligence with the steps by which it was immediately followed.   Mr. Anderton at once received an intimation of the Baron's approaching departure for the continent, and at the end of the third week from that time leave was taken, and he apparently started upon his journey.   In point of fact, however, his plans were of a very different character.   During the three weeks which intervened between his visit to Doctor's Commons and his farewell to Mr. Anderton, there had been advertised in the parish church of Kensington the banns

of marriage between himself and his " medium," Rosalie,—not, indeed, in the names by which they were ordinarily known, and which
would very probably have excited attention, but in the family name—
if so it be—of the Baron and in that by which Rosalie was originally
known when with the travelling circus. By what means he prevailed
upon his victim to consent to such a step is not important to the matter
in hand. The general tenour of the subsequent evidence shows clearly
that it must have been under some form of compulsion, and, indeed,
the unfortunate girl seems to have been made by some means altogether
subservient to his will.

The marriage thus secretly effected, the Baron and his wife leave
town, not for the continent, as stated to Mr. Anderton, but for Bognor,
an out-of-the-way little watering-place on the Sussex coast, deserted
save for the week of the Goodwood races, where, at that time of the
year, he was not likely to meet with any one to whom he was known.
Before endeavouring to investigate the motive of all this mystery, it
is necessary to bear in mind one important fact :—

*Between the wife of Baron R** and Mr. Wilson's legacy of 25,000l.,
the lives of Mr. and Mrs. Anderton now alone intervened.*

The first few days of the Baron's stay in Bognor seem to have been
devoted to the search for a servant, he having insisted on the unusual
arrangement of himself providing one in the house where he lodged.
It is worthy of note that the one finally selected was in a position, with
respect to character, that placed her entirely in her master's power.
It is unfortunate that this same defect of character necessarily lessens
the value of evidence from such a source. We must, however, take it
for what it is worth, remembering at the same time, that there is a total
absence of any apparent motive, save that of telling the truth, for the
statement she has made.

It appears, then, from her account, that after trying by every means
to tempt her into some repetition of her former error, the Baron at last
seized upon the pretext of her taking from the breakfast table a single
taste of jam upon her finger, to threaten her with immediate and utter
ruin. One only loop-hole was left by which she could escape. The
alternative was, indeed, most ingeniously and delicately veiled under
the pretext of seeking a plausible reason for her dismissal ; but, in
point of fact, it amounted to this, that as a condition of her alleged
offence not being recorded against her, she would own to the commission
of another with which she had nothing whatever to do.

The offence to which she was falsely to plead guilty was this. On
the night succeeding the commission of the fault of which, such as it
was, she was really guilty, Madame R** was taken suddenly ill. The
symptoms were those of antimonial poisoning. The presence of
antimony in the stomach was clearly shown. In the presence of the
medical man who had been called in, the girl was taxed by the Baron
with having administered, by way of a trick, a dose of tartar emetic ;
and she, in obedience to a strong hint from her master, confessed to

the delinquency, and was thereupon dismissed with a good character in other respects. Freed from the dread of exposure, she now flatly denies the whole affair, both of the trick and of the quarrel which was supposed to have led to it, and I am bound to say, that looking both to external and internal evidence, her statement seems worthy of credit.

Nevertheless the poison was unquestionably administered. By whom ?

Cui bono ? Certainly, it will be said, not for that of the Baron; for until at least the death of Mr. and Mrs. Anderton his interest was clearly in the life of his wife. It is not, therefore, by any means to be supposed that he would before that event attempt to poison her. Of this mystery, then, it appears that we must seek the solution elsewhere.

III

Returning then for a time to Mr. and Mrs. Anderton, we find that the latter has also suffered from an attack of illness. Comparing her journal and the evidence of her doctor, with that given in the case of Madame R**, it appears that the symptoms were identical in every respect, with this single but important exception, that in this case there is no apparent cause for the attack, nor can any trace of poison be found. A little further inquiry, and we arrive at a yet more mysterious coincidence.

It is a matter of universal experience, that almost the most fatal enemy of crime is over-precaution. In this particular case the precautions of the Baron R** appear to have been dictated by a skill and forethought almost superhuman, and so admirably have they been taken, that, save in the concealment of the marriage, it is almost impossible to recognise in them any sinister motive whatever. His course with respect to the servant girl, though dictated, as we believe, by the most criminal designs, is perfectly consistent with motives of the very highest philanthropy. Even in the concealment of the marriage, once granting—as I think may very fairly be granted—that such a marriage might be concealed without any necessary imputation of evil, the means adopted were equally simple, effective, and unblameable. They consisted merely in the use of the real, instead of the stage names of the contracting parties, and in the very proper avoidance of all ground for scandal by hiring another lodging, in order that before marriage the address of both parties might not be the same. In the illness of Madame R**, too, at Bognor, nothing can, to all appearance, be more straightforward than the Baron's conduct. He at once proclaims his suspicion of poison, sends for an eminent physician, verifies his doubts, administers the proper remedies, and dismisses the servant by whose fault the attack has been occasioned. Viewed with an eye of suspicion, there is indeed something questionable in the selection of the medical attendant. Why should the Baron refuse to send for either of the local practitioners, both gentlemen of skill and reputation, and insist on calling in a stranger to the place, who in a very few days would leave it, and very probably return no more? Distrust of country doctors, and decided preference for London skill, furnishes us, as usual, with a prompt and plausible reply. It does not, however, exclude the possibility that the expediency of removing as far as possible all evidence of what had passed may have in some degree affected the choice. Be that as it may, this precaution, whether originally for good or for evil, has enabled us to fix with certainty a very important point.

Mrs. Anderton was taken ill, not only with the same symptoms, but at the same time, with Madame R**.

Before proceeding to consider the events which followed, there are one or two points in the history of this first illness of the sisters on which it is needful to remark. The action of these metallic poisons, among which we may undoubtedly rank antimony, is as yet but very little understood. We know, however, from the statements of Professor Taylor,* certainly by far the first English authority upon the subject, that peculiarities of constitution, or, as they are termed, " idiosyncracies," frequently assist or impede to a very extraordinary extent the action of such drugs. The constitution of Madame R** appears to have been thus idiosyncratically disposed to favour the action of antimony. There can be no doubt that the action of the poison upon her system was very greatly in excess of that which under ordinary circumstances would have been expected from a similar dose. The poison, therefore, by whomsoever administered, was not intended to prove fatal, though from the peculiar idiosyncracy of Madame R** it was very nearly doing so.

The narrowness of Madame R**'s escape seems to have struck the Baron, and to have exercised a strong influence over his future proceedings. Whether or not he knew or believed her to be exposed to any peculiar influences which might tend to render her life less secure than that of her delicate and invalid sister, it is impossible positively to say. There was no question, however, that her death before that of Mrs. Anderton would destroy all prospect of his succession to the 25,000*l.*, and with this view he proceeded to take as speedily as possible the necessary steps to secure himself against such an event. The obvious course, and indeed that suggested at once by Dr. Jones, was that of assurance, and this course he accordingly adopted, after having previously, by a tour of several months, restored his wife to a state of health in which her life would probably be accepted by the offices concerned. The insurances, therefore, with which we are concerned, were effected in consequence of a previous administration of poison to Madame R**, producing an illness far more serious than could have been anticipated, and accompanied by precisely similar symptoms on the part of her delicate sister, Mrs. Anderton, whose death, *if preceding that of Madame R***, would more than double the Baron's prospect of succession.

* " Taylor on Poisons," 2nd edition, p. 98, *et inf.*

Between him, therefore, and the sum of either 25,000*l.* or 50,000*l.* there now intervened three lives, those of Mr. and Mrs. Anderton, and of his own wife, Madame R**, and on the order in which they fell depended the amount of his gain by their demise. The death of Mr. Anderton before that of Mrs. Anderton, would open the possibility of a second marriage, from which might arise issue, whose claim would precede his; that of his own wife preceding that of either Mr. or Mrs. Anderton, would destroy altogether his own claim to the larger sum. It was only in the event of Mrs. Anderton's death being followed first by that of her husband, and afterwards by that of her sister, that Baron's entire claim would be secured.

Within one year from the time at which matters assumed this position, these three lives fell in, and in precisely the order in which the Baron would most largely and securely profit by their demise.

We now proceed to examine the circumstances under which they fell.

Immediately on his return to England, and before apparently completing his arrangements with respect to the policies of insurance, the Baron, we find, calls upon Mr. Anderton, and by dint of minute inquiries draws from him the entire history of the attack from which Mrs. Anderton had suffered several months before. Supposing, therefore, that the information was of any practical interest, the Baron was now fully aware of the perfect similarity, both of time and symptom, between the cases of his wife and her sister. It is essential that this should be borne in mind.

V

He now proceeds to establish himself in lodgings in Russell Plac e in a house in which, for five days and every night in the week, he is entirely alone. The only other tenant is a medical man, whose visits are confined to a few hours on two days in the week, and who lives at too great a distance to be called in on any sudden emergency. Here he establishes himself upon the first and second floors with a laboratory in a small detached room upon the basement floor, where his chemical experiments can be carried on without inconvenience to the rest of the house. It is essential that the position of this laboratory should be very clearly borne in mind, as it plays a most important part in the story which is now to follow.

In these lodgings, then, Madame R** is again taken ill with a return, though in a greatly mitigated form, of the same symptoms from which she had previously suffered at Bognor. The attack, however, though less violent in its immediate effects, was succeeded at regular intervals of about a fortnight by others of a precisely similar character. And here we arrive at what is at once the most significant, the most extraordinary, and the most questionable of the evidence we have been able to collect.

VII

It appears, then, that upon a night in August, a young man of the name of Aldridge, who, as a matter of special favour, had been taken into the house since the arrival of the Baron, saw Madame R** leave her bedroom, and, apparently in her sleep, walk down the stairs in the dark to the lower part of the house. The room in which the Baron slept was next to hers, and on the wall of that room, projected by the night-lamp burning on the table, the young man saw what seemed to be the shadow of a man watching Madame R** as she went by. He looked again and the shadow was gone—so rapidly that at first he could scarcely believe his eyes, and was only, after consideration, satisfied that it really had been there. He went down to the room, but the Baron was asleep. He told him what had happened to Madame R**, and he at once followed her. Young Aldridge watched him until he had descended the kitchen-stairs and returned, followed closely by the sleep-walker. He then went back to his room, to which the Baron shortly afterwards came to thank him for his warning, and to tell him that, in some freak of slumber, Madame R** *had visited the kitchen.*

So far the story is simple enough. There is nothing extraordinary in a sick woman of exciteable nerves taking a sudden fit of somnambulism, and walking down even into the kitchen of a house that was not her own. The Baron's conduct—in all respects but that of the watching shadow—was precisely that which, from a sensible and affectionate husband, might most naturally have been expected. Nor is it very difficult, even setting aside all idea of malice, to set down the shadow portion of the story to a mere freak of imagination on the part of the young man who, though " not drunk," was nevertheless on his own admission, " perhaps a little excited," and who had been "drinking a good deal of beer and shandy-gaff." But the evidence does not end here.

By one of those extraordinary coincidences by which the simple course of ordinary events so often baffles the best laid schemes of crime, there were others in the house, besides the young man Aldridge, who witnessed the movements of the Baron and Madame R**. It so happened that, on the afternoon of that particular day, the woman of the house had hampered the little latch-lock by which young Aldridge usually admitted himself, and, as this occurred late in the day, it is more than probable that the Baron was unaware of it, as also of the fact that in consequence the servant-girl Susan Turner, sat up beyond the usual hour of going to bed for the purpose of letting the young man in. This girl, it seems, had a lover—a stoker on one of the northern lines—and him she appears to have invited to keep her company on her watch. Aldridge returned and went up to bed, but the lover— who was to be on duty with his engine at two o'clock, and who was doubtlessly interrupted in a most interesting conversation by the arrival of the lodger—still remained in the kitchen, and was only just leaving it when Madame R** came down stairs. Taking her at first to be the mistress of the house, and fearful lest the street-lamp gleaming through the glass partition should betray her " young man's " presence, Susan Turner draws him to the lumber-room, the window of which, it appears, looks into a sort of well between the house and the two rooms built out at the back, after a fashion not unusual in London houses. Into this well, also, immediately opposite to the window of the lumber-room, looks that of the backroom or laboratory, furnished with what the witness describes as a " tin looking-glass " but which is really one of those metal reflectors, in common use, for increasing the light of rooms in such a position. The distance between the two windows is little more than eight feet. The night was clear, with a bright, full harvest moon, and its rays, thrown by the reflector into the laboratory, made every part of its interior distinctly visible from the lumber-room. The door of the latter room was open, and the staircase illuminated by the Baron's approaching light. The hiders in the lumber-room could see distinctly the whole proceedings of both Baron and Madame R**, from the time Aldridge lost sight of them to the moment they again emerged into his view.

And this was what they saw :

" *Madame R** never went into the kitchen at all ;* " " *she went straight into the laboratory,*" and " *the Baron watched her as she came out.*"

A glance at the place will show the bearing of this evidence and the impossibility of the Baron (who, if he had not been in the kitchen, must at least have thoroughly known the position of his own laboratory) having made any mistake on this point.

What, then, was his motive in thus imposing upon Aldridge, to whose interference he professed himself so much indebted, with this false statement of the place to which Madame R** had been ?

There does not seem the slightest reason for discrediting the evidence of these two witnesses. Their story is perfectly simple and coherent. There is neither malice against the Baron nor collusion with Aldridge, in whose case such malice is supposed to exist. The only weak point in their position is the fact, that they were both doing wrong in being in that place at that time ; but the admission of this, in truth, rather strengthens than injures the testimony which involves it. We must seek the clue, then, not in their motives, but in those of the Baron. The errand of Madame R**, in her strange expedition, may perhaps afford it. What did she do in the laboratory ?

" *She drank something from a bottle.*" " *It smelt and tasted like sherry.*" " *It was marked* VIN. ANT. POT. TART." *That label designates antimonial wine, which is a mixture of sherry and tartar emetic.*

Let us see if from this point we can feel our way, as it were, backwards, to the motive for concealment. The life of Madame R** was, as we know, heavily insured. It had already been seriously endangered by the effects of precisely the same drug as that she was now seen to take. If the Baron knew or suspected the motive of her visit, here is at once a motive sufficient, if not perhaps very creditable, for the concealment of a fact, the knowledge of which might very probably lead to difficulty with respect to payment of the policy in case of death.

But here another difficulty meets us. The incident in question occurred at about the middle of the long illness of Madame R**. That illness consisted of a series of attacks, occurring as nearly as possible at intervals of a fortnight, and exhibiting the exact symptoms of the poison here shown to have been taken. One of these attacks followed within a very few hours of the occurrence into which we are examining. Was it the only one of the kind?

The evidence of the night-nurse bears with terrible weight upon this point. Her orders are strict, on no account to close her eyes. Her hours of watch are short, and the repose of the entire day leaves her without the slightest cause for unusual drowsiness. The testimonials of twenty years bear unvarying witness to her care and trustworthiness. Yet every alternate Saturday for eight or ten, or it may even have been nearly twelve weeks, at one regular hour she falls asleep. It is in vain that she watches and fights against it—in vain even that, suspecting " some trick " she on one occasion abstains entirely from food, and drinks nothing but that peculiarly wakeful decoction, strong green tea. On every other night she keeps awake with ease, but surely as the fatal Saturday comes round she again succumbs, and surely as sleep steals over her is it followed by a fresh attack of the symptoms we so plainly recognise. She cannot in any way account for such an extraordinary fatality. She is positive that such a thing never happened to her before. We also are at an equal loss. We can but pause upon the reflection that twice before the periodic drowsiness began, a similarly irresistible sleep had been induced by the so-called mesmeric powers of the Baron himself. And then we pass naturally to her who had been for years habituated to such control, and we cannot but call to mind the statement of Mr. Hands—" I have often *willed* her (S. Parsons) to go into a dark room and pick up a pin, or some article equally minute."

And then we again remember the watching shadow on the wall.

And yet, after all, at what have we arrived? Grant that the Baron knew the nature of his wife's errand in the laboratory; that the singular power—call it what we will—by which he had before in jest compelled the nurse to sleep, was really employed in enabling the somnambulist to elude her watch. Grant even that the pretensions of the mesmerist are true, and that it was in obedience to his direct will that Madame R** acted as she did, we are no nearer a solution than before.

It was not the Baron's interest that his wife should die.

We must then seek further afield for any explanation of this terrible enigma. Let us see how it fared with Mrs. Anderton while these events were passing at her sister's house.

III and V

And heie we seem to have another instance of the manner in which the wisest precautions so often turn against those by whom they are taken. Admitting that the illness of Madame R** was really caused by criminal means, nothing could be wiser than the precaution which selected for their first essay a night on which they could be tried without fear of observation. Yet this very circumstance, enables us to fix a date of the last importance, which without it must have remained uncertain. Madame R**, then, was taken ill on Saturday, the 5th April. On that very night—at, as nearly as can be ascertained, the very same hour, Mrs. Anderton was unaccountably seized with an illness in all respects resembling hers. Like hers, too, the attacks returned at fortnightly intervals. For a few days, on the Baron's advice, a particular medicine is given, and at first with apparently good effect. At the same date the diary of Dr. Marsden shows a similar amelioration of symptoms in the case of Madame R**. In both cases the amendment is but short, and the disease again pursues its course. The result in both is utter exhaustion. In the case of Madame R** reducing the sufferer to death's door ; in the *weaker constitution* of her sister terminating in death. Examination is made. The appearances of the body, no less than the symptoms exhibited in life, are all those of antimonial poisoning. No antimony is, however, found ; and from this and other circumstances, results a verdict of " Natural Death." On the 12th October, then, Mrs. Anderton's story ends.

*From that time dates the recovery of Madame R**.*

VI

The first life is now removed from between Baron R** and the full sum of 50,000l. Let us examine briefly the circumstances attending the lapse of the second. Here again events each in itself quite simple and natural, combine to form a story fraught with terrible suspicion. I have alluded to the inquest which followed on the death of Mrs. Anderton. That inquiry originated in circumstances which cast upon her husband the entire suspicion of her murder. To whose agency, whether direct or indirect, voluntary or involuntary, is an after question, may every one of these circumstances be traced ? Mr. Anderton insists on being the only one from whom the patient shall receive either medicine or food. It is the Baron who applauds and encourages a line of conduct diametrically opposed to his own, and tending more than any other circumstance to fix suspicion on his friend. A remedy is suggested, the recommending of which points strongly to the idea of poison, and it is from the Baron that the suggestion comes. Two papers are found, the one bearing in part the other in full, the name of the poison suspected to have been used. The first of these is brought to light by the Baron himself,—the second is found in a place where he has just been, and by a person whom he has himself despatched to search there for something else. He draws continual attention to that point of exclusive attendance from which suspicion chiefly springs. His replies to Dr. Dodsworth respecting the recommendation of the antimonial antidote are so given as to confirm the worst interpretation to which it had given rise, and even when, on the discovery of the second paper, he advises the nurse that it should be destroyed, he does so in a manner that ensures not only its preservation but its immediate employment in the manner most dangerous to his friend.

The evidence fails. What is the Baron's connection with the catastrophe that follows? He knows well the accused man's nervous anxiety for his own good name. He procures, on the ground of his friendly anxiety, the earliest intelligence of his friends' probable acquittal. He enters that friend's room to acquaint him with the good news. Returning he takes measures to secure the prisoner throughout the night from interruption or interference. In the morning Mr. Anderton is a corpse, and on his pillow is found the phial in which the poison had been contained, and a written statement that the desperate step had been taken in despair of an acquittal. By what marvellous accident was the hopeful news of the chemical investigation thus misinterpreted? By what negligence or connivance was the fatal drug placed with his reach? One thing only we know—

It was the Baron who conveyed the news. It was from his pocket medicine case, left by him within the sick man's reach, that the poison came.

Thus fell the second of the two lives which stood between the Baron and the full sum of 50,000*l*. Of this sum the 25,000*l*. which accrues from the relationship between Mrs. Anderton and Madame R** is already his as soon as claimed, but there is no immediate necessity for the claim to be preferred. He may perhaps have thought it better to wait before making such a claim until the first sensation occasioned by the double deaths through which he inherited had passed away. He may have been merely putting in train some plausible story to account for his only now proclaiming a fact of which he had certainly been aware for at least a year. Whatever his reason, however, he certainly for some weeks after Mr. Anderton's death made no movement to establish his claim upon the property, and during this time Madame R** was slowly but surely recovering her strength.

But while wisdom thus dictated a policy of delay, the irresistible course of events hurried on the crisis. A letter comes filled with threats of the vengeance of jealous love if its cause be not that night removed. It is but a fragment of that letter that is preserved, but its meaning is clear enough, and it is that the connection between himself and Madame R** should be finally brought to an end.

VII

" N'en sais-tu bien le moyen ? "

That night the condition is fulfilled. Once more the sleeping lady takes her midnight journey to her husband's laboratory. Once more her unconscious hand pours out the deadly draught. But this time it is no slow poison that she takes. It is a powerful and burning acid that even as it awakes her from her trance, shrivels her with a horrible and instant death. One shrill and quickly stifled shriek alarms the inmates of the house, and when they hurry to the spot they find only a disfigured corpse, lying with bare feet and disordered night dress in the darkness of the stormy November night, and with the fatal glass still clasped in its hand.

My task is done. In possession of the evidence thus placed before you, your judgment of its result will be as good as mine. Link by link you have now been put in possession of the entire chain. Is that chain one of purely accidental coincidences, or does it point with terrible certainty to a series of crimes, in their nature and execution almost too horrible to contemplate ? That is the first question to be asked, and it is one to which I confess myself unable to reply. The second is more strange, and perhaps even more difficult still. Supposing the latter to be the case, are crimes thus committed susceptible of proof, or even if proved, are they of a kind for which the criminal can be brought to punishment ?

Literature of Mystery and Detection

AN ARNO PRESS COLLECTION

Lynch, Lawrence L. (pseud. of Emma Murdoch Van Deventer). **Dangerous Ground.** 1885

Meade, L. T. (pseud. of Elizabeth Thomasina Smith) and Clifford Halifax. **Stories From the Diary of a Doctor.** 1895

Moffett, Cleveland. **Through the Wall.** [1909]

Morrison, Arthur. **Martin Hewitt, Investigator.** [1894]

O. Henry (pseud. of William Sidney Porter). **The Gentle Grafter.** 1908

Orczy, [Emmuska]. **Lady Molly of Scotland Yard.** [1926]

Payn, James. **Lost Sir Massingberd.** [n. d.]

Pemberton, Max. **Jewel Mysteries I Have Known.** [1894]

Pidgin, Charles Felton and J. M. Taylor. **The Chronicles of Quincy Adams Sawyer, Detective.** 1912

Pinkerton, Allan. **The Expressman and the Detective.** 1875

Post, Melville Davisson. **The Strange Schemes of Randolph Mason.** [1896]

Reeve, Arthur B[enjamin]. **The Silent Bullet.** 1912

Shiel, M[atthew] P[hipps]. **Prince Zaleski.** 1895

[Simms, William Gilmore]. **Martin Faber, The Story of a Criminal; and Other Tales.** 1837. Two volumes in one

Speight, T[homas] W[ilkinson]. **Under Lock and Key.** 1869. Three volumes in one

Stevenson, Burton E[gbert]. **The Mystery of the Boule Cabinet.** 1921

Trollope, T[homas] Adolphus. **A Siren.** 1870. Three volumes in one

[Vidocq, Eugène François]. **Memoirs of Vidocq. Principal Agent of the French Police Until 1827.** 1828/1829. Four volumes in two

Warren, Samuel. **Experiences of a Barrister, and Confessions of an Attorney.** 1859. Two volumes in one

"Waters" (pseud. of William Russell). **The.Experiences of a French Detective Officer** .[185?]

Whyte-Melville, G[eorge] J[ohn]. **M. Or N.** 1869. Two volumes in one

DATE DUE